CAINE HOUSE

An Emmie Rose Haunted Mystery Book 2

DEAN RASMUSSEN

Caine House: An Emmie Rose Haunted Mystery Book 2

Dean Rasmussen

For more information about this book, visit:

www.deanrasmussen.com
dean@deanrasmussen.com

Caine House: An Emmie Rose Haunted Mystery Book 2

Published by:

Dark Venture Press, 601 Central Ave W, Ste 103 #129, Saint Michael, MN 55376

Cover Art: Mibl Art

Developmental Editor: C.B. Moore

Line Editor: C.B. Moore

❀ Created with Vellum

S omething had gone wrong. Horribly wrong.

"I did it right," Shannon Fisher insisted. "I did exactly as the book instructed."

"You must have missed something," Eddie said.

She held the book open in her lap and flipped through the pages, shaking her head. "No, I read it word for word. I was so careful."

"Maybe the pronunciation is more important than we thought."

"I'm sure I said it right."

Her husband leaned forward and adjusted his hands on the steering wheel as they sped toward the exit. It was straight ahead, but the narrow, winding path prevented a quick escape. No posted speed limit, but who'd be crazy enough to race through a cemetery at night? So many trees among the shadows, and gravestones only inches from the edge of the road—one mistake and it would all be over.

The tires thumped against something hard at the edge of the road.

"Careful," she begged.

"It's hard to see."

Speeding out the front gate, Eddie didn't pause to check for cross-traffic on the main road. Shannon checked her peripheral vision for him—no cars anywhere. They turned right, racing down the street a block before making another sharp right turn down a winding gravel road leading out to the safety of the countryside.

With the open road ahead, she took a deep breath, but he kept speeding up as rocks cracked against the belly of the car. A pothole appeared ahead. Too late—he slammed over it, jarring the car to the side as something metal broke loose. The muffler?

He'd damaged the car, but it didn't matter. They just needed to get out of there.

Eddie looked behind them through the rearview mirror. "Wouldn't the iron gate keep it contained?"

"I don't think that's how it works." The book jumped in her hands, and she craned her head around to look out the rear window. "I think it's out."

"No, no, no," her husband muttered, pushing his foot down on the gas. "Is it keeping up? Can we outrun it?"

"I don't know."

She gripped the book hard, trying to keep it still so she could read. Had she missed a word or mispronounced something? All the preparation—repeating the lines over and over. Still, she had failed to contain it, and she blamed herself. What had she done wrong?

The shadow approached in the side mirror, silhouetted in the streetlights and the moon's ambient glow across the surrounding countryside. She opened her mouth but held back a shriek.

"Shannon!" her husband cried.

She knew he wanted to reach for her hand and couldn't, but she needed him to focus on the road. The twisted shadow following them would tear them apart if they couldn't outrun it. The thought sent chills up her spine. They had tried to stop it, and now it was furious.

Hitting a patch of loose gravel, the car lost traction and slid over the road's edge, bumping along the grassy ditch for several seconds before Eddie steered it back onto the road. Shannon gasped, her gaze jumping from the road ahead, to the book, to the side mirror.

But it had *seen* them. No chance of outrunning it forever. Spirits like this rarely gave up on their own.

"We shouldn't have done it alone." Eddie winced.

That was clear now, but they'd had no choice.

Eddie peered into the mirror. "Oh, shit! It's catching up."

She closed her eyes and recited the lines from memory this time. She shouted at them. They were correct.

The wavering shadow appeared in her mirror again, showing no signs of slowing or dispersing as it should, barreling through like a churning ball of black smoke, and Eddie stepped on the gas despite the loose gravel threatening to toss the car off the road. The spirit increased its speed, but all they could do was race ahead of it...

Another car whizzed by, going in the opposite direction. She watched it head straight into the black cloud, but the driver made no attempt to slow or move out of the way. They hadn't seen the horror creeping up.

She slammed her hand against the dashboard. "Then why the hell isn't it working?"

It wasn't supposed to be like this. Everything they had trained for had failed, despite years of practice. Her heart ached that she couldn't make it right. It would never be right because...

She wasn't the powerful psychic in the family.

"Emmie..." she mumbled, her eyes filling with tears.

Eddie half-glanced at her. "She's safe, at least."

The form moved closer now, only a couple of car lengths behind them. In a few seconds it would touch their car, and then what? Would it consume their souls or drag them to hell? She had repeated so many times to Emmie that the spirits couldn't hurt her. Dread passed through her chest, a toxic, sickening dread, as she wished she had never lied to her daughter like that.

Wished she'd never put her poor girl through all the pain and suffering, despite the motive.

The dark form stretched out wide limbs along both sides of the car as if it would embrace them. Shannon could almost make out the face and its evil eyes peering at her through the glass.

The intersection where they needed to turn right appeared ahead, threatening to slow them down again and give the pursuer that last bit of advantage they held. She calculated in those few seconds how fast Eddie could take the turn without losing control. The inside corner sloped down at a sharp angle, so if he hugged the entire inner corner, taking advantage of the low banking, and then allowed himself a wide arc, veering across into the other lane for a short distance, he could make the turn, as long as no cars came from the other direction. *If* everything went right.

Eddie hit the corner hard, but the car slid straight through the intersection. The tail whipped to the side, and he struggled to stay on the road now. He fought against the steering wheel as the car veered to the center of the road again.

He missed the turn.

"Eddie!" Her heart pounded in her ears.

Letting off the gas only seconds before the turn, the engine wound down as the speedometer plummeted. The delay allowed the impending shadow to envelop the driver's side window. Inside, the car darkened as if the deepest night had come. Only the light coming in through the windshield led the way.

The car hit the corner too close to the inside edge. It skidded and slammed down into the steep slope, scraping the car's underside through the gravel, then bounced up across the road to the right. Eddie jerked the steering wheel to the side, maneuvering it as if skidding on winter ice as they'd done so many times before—but this time it slipped through his hands for a moment and he lost control. He slammed the wheel in the other direction to compensate for the error, but the momentum took over.

Everything slowed. A cat jumped out in slow motion from the brush along the edge of the road. Red fur and a collar. Probably a stray farm cat. Poor thing darted out in front of them. *Why do animals always do that?* Eddie cranked the wheel to avoid hitting it, and the car slid sideways in a cloud of darkness and dust before hitting the edge of the ditch and flipping over again and again, as if tumbling through a clothes dryer.

The smell of gas filled the air, and the book slammed into her face before the car stopped rolling. They came to a rest, hanging upside down with their arms dangling limp. A harsh cold breeze blew in through the shattered windows. Only darkness now, as blood drained from Eddie's unconscious face.

"Eddie?" Shannon reached out to him as a presence gripped her and squeezed.

It wasn't possible—a lie. Her brain was playing tricks on her.

"They can't hurt you," she whispered, as she had whispered to Emmie so many times. *Oh, they could hurt her all right, but if she was strong enough, it wouldn't hurt too bad.*

It hurt really bad now.

Eddie gasped and stopped breathing as Shannon floated on the edge of consciousness and closed her eyes.

"I'm so sorry, Emmie."

2

E mmie brushed off her hands and scanned the piles of boxes and remnants of her childhood in the garage. Her inheritance.

"It doesn't look like we've done anything." Sarah took in a deep breath.

"It's going to take longer than I thought."

Sarah laughed. "Good times. Living with you is an adventure, that's for sure. More stuff happened to me in a month than in years."

"Back at you, kid," Emmie said, laughing as well. "And you're the only roommate who will put up with the ghosts. You've met them all."

"And then some."

Emmie stood with Sarah near the garage's open door. They had only gone through a tenth of the items before pausing for a few minutes.

"I never knew my parents had all these odds and ends lying around. Maybe I should have thrown out all the stuff that wasn't sold in the auction a long time ago and saved us the trouble."

"It's better to double check. You don't want to accidentally throw out something valuable or sentimental."

"I guess."

Some things they'd found represented fond memories for Emmie, like souvenirs from childhood family trips and Halloween decorations—plenty of those—and a few boxes of clothes she had worn in high school. There was an old footstool she had sat on many times, at the feet of her dad as he lay back in his recliner and read his books. One box held three antique paintings of such macabre subjects that it was no wonder nobody had purchased them. Who would want a large artwork depicting a city of skulls hanging on their living room wall? How much had her parents spent on that one?

Truly, most of it was nothing anyone would ever want, especially considering the history of the house. Maybe someone out there would jump at the chance to own an authentic 1956 Ouija board, but unless they showed up soon, it would most likely end up in the trash.

She'd come home to face an empty house and the Hanging Girl, but scavenging through the boxes and plastic totes now only brought more painful childhood memories that she had pushed aside for years. The last of her past sat in front of her, and she had the choice to either throw it all in a dumpster and walk away or pick through it one last time. She couldn't quite bring herself to choose the dumpster, not when she was still working through the mysteries in her past and the things they had recently been through.

She hoped Sarah wasn't regretting her decision to help because it was hard work, both physically and emotionally, and Sarah was delicate at the moment. Each box they opened meant Emmie had to face another part of her past.

"I don't think we can finish this in one day," Sarah said.

"Doesn't look that way."

"It doesn't matter, we'll still make it."

Sarah pulled one of the purple plastic totes off the pile and placed it at her feet. Opening the lid, she found no surprises. Just another Ouija board and several more oversized hardcover books. "How many of these did your parents have?"

"Way too many."

Most of the items had been haphazardly placed into the totes after John and Mary had organized the auction years earlier. They had done their best to keep things sorted, putting everything back into some sense of order within the garage. On one side sat all the occult and freaky shit nobody would ever buy, and on the other, leftover pots and pans, clothes, household items, and her dad's automotive repair items.

"You could donate what you don't use," Sarah suggested.

"I'd hate to discover that some careless purchaser accidentally summoned a demon with the wrong thing."

Sarah stopped and laughed, and it brought another smile to Emmie's face. It was good to see her happy.

"What are we going to do with this?" Sarah lifted out a long necklace and examined it. "Are these pearls?" She studied them closer and cringed. "Ugh, are these human teeth?"

"Probably."

"Funny that it didn't sell in the auction."

"I wouldn't be surprised to find a full skeleton in all of this."

"We could open up our own psychic emporium. Psychics R Us."

"That's not a bad idea." Emmie laughed.

Sarah returned the necklace and dug through a handful of other items before pushing the tote aside. She flipped an empty tote upside down and sat, watching Emmie open yet another one.

Emmie paused and met her eyes. "Are you tired?"

"A little, but don't worry about it. It's okay. It helps me keep my mind off my grandmother."

Emmie nodded. "We'll just take it easy."

"Life is full of surprises, I guess. At least she still has that spark in her eyes, and I know she can understand me, but I can't even imagine what my grandmother is going through with all her strong opinions and wisdom. It was so wonderful to see her yesterday, but I did all the talking. She could barely stay awake. The doctor said she might not make it another week."

"Well, she's lucky she has a nurse for a granddaughter. How are your parents handling it?"

"They take turns visiting with her, but they can only be there for a few hours at a time because of their jobs. I'll probably visit her after I'm done here."

"Yes, absolutely. I completely understand. Don't worry about me in all this..." Emmie looked around. "... junk."

This brought a smile back to Sarah's face.

"Let's take a break." Emmie grabbed one large box on the household items side of the garage near the door and carried it outside. Someone had written "Recovered" across one side in black marker. No other boxes were labeled, and she was curious, but she could go through it inside the house. It was probably an old set of plates or kitchen appliances, and they might come in handy considering the state of her finances.

They circled around the house to the front door. Cloudy skies had moved in, and the wind picked up a little, but the temperature hovered in the mid-seventies. Early September weather was perfect for scavenging through the garage. Another month or two and it would be too cold to spend over thirty minutes out there.

They walked into the house and Emmie dropped the box on the counter while Sarah retreated to Mary's old apartment, where she had set up her bedroom in Frankie's old room. The nighttime fears had disappeared after calling a truce with the Hanging Girl.

It was beneficial to share the house with Sarah. Splitting the costs would allow Emmie time to get back on her feet financially while she gathered freelance work, and Sarah could shed the burden of an overpriced apartment. A perfect match for their very odd situation.

Sarah returned a few minutes later, followed by Alice Hyde,

the Hanging Girl.

"She's behind me, isn't she?" Sarah asked.

"Right on your heels."

"I don't like the color," Alice said.

Emmie turned to Sarah. "I don't think turquoise is Alice's favorite color."

Sarah frowned. "Tell her I'm sorry, but turquoise helps to calm me. Just like a blue sky or the ocean."

"I prefer pink," Alice said. "Tell her to paint it all pink."

"Alice wants you to paint her apartment pink."

"Pink? I'm twenty-six, not thirteen. Maybe I can put up some pink curtains along one wall."

Alice cringed.

Emmie grinned. "I don't think she likes your decorating decisions."

"I can play a song on the piano for her later on, if that helps. What song does she want me to play this time?"

"All of them," Alice answered.

"Take your pick," Emmie said to Sarah.

Alice stood between them and stared as they went about their lunch break. Despite the trauma that Alice had suffered in death, she still didn't want Sarah or Emmie to help her. It was Alice's house, and they were merely guests. Emmie did everything possible to make their host happy. She had seen what Alice was capable of doing when she lost her patience.

After lunch, Sarah opened a tote on the kitchen floor, one that she had carried in earlier that morning, and pulled out an ornate lamp with a skull as its base. She held it out at arm's length toward Emmie. "Here, you can put this in your room."

Emmie took it from her. "Oh, thanks. I like that grin. And knowing my parents, it might be someone I met."

She formed a confused expression while removing jumper cables, a tool set, several coat hangers, and several road maps before stopping when someone knocked at the door.

Emmie got up, dusted off her hands on her jeans, and

answered it. Finn stood in the doorway with his devious smile.

"Welcome back!" Emmie held the door open for him as he stepped inside. He hugged her.

"The traveler returns," Sarah cried, getting up from the floor and moving toward him. She embraced him. "How was Japan?"

"*Subarashī*. That means awesome in Japanese," he said.

"Show-off." Emmie chuckled and closed the door behind him.

"Well, if you liked that one, here's another. I'll probably mispronounce it." With his arm still around Sarah's shoulder, he stared into her eyes and added, "*Kanojo no me wa utsukushikatta desu...*"

Sarah blinked while Emmie closed the door and followed them. "Uh-oh, that sounds suspicious."

"It means *she had beautiful eyes*." He smirked.

"Had?" Sarah asked.

"You girls want too much from me," he said in mock distress. "Though I can also ask, 'Where is the bathroom?'"

"Want a drink before the bathroom?" Emmie asked wryly.

Soon they were sitting around the kitchen table, a place which had served them well as a meeting point before, sipping their beers from the bottle. Finn told them about his trip and took out a couple of small boxes from his pocket, which he pushed toward them. They found something wrapped in little black cloth bags inside, red for Emmie and blue for Sarah.

"Omamori," Finn said. "Good luck charms for your wallet or pocket or for below your pillows."

Emmie refrained from grimacing at yet another charm or amulet or anything mystical, but she gave him a bright, thankful smile instead.

"I was just saying how much I love turquoise." Sarah's pleasant expression faded after turning back toward the living room. "Except that Alice doesn't like it much."

His eyes widened and followed hers. "Is she here?"

"I don't see her now." Emmie glanced around. "But I'm sure

she's listening." She couldn't help enjoying Finn's audible gulp.

"Doesn't she frighten you guys anymore?"

"Not after what happened last month," Sarah said. "The harsh feelings are gone now, and we get along."

"You missed some wonderful moments back here." Emmie watched his reaction, hoping he might regret going off to Japan a little. "Some great opportunities for your research. Sarah and I released four child spirits from around this area. Three boys and a girl—if you could have seen the joy on their faces..."

Sarah's face brightened. "It took Emmie a few days to get one boy to speak about his attachment to an old tree near the edge of a field a few miles away. The boy had died there in a house fire decades ago, and he wouldn't let go of that tree—it was the last recognizable piece of his earthly life—but he finally talked with her. He was so confused at first, but he let us lead him home."

Finn nodded slowly. "I guess I've got a lot to learn about the spirit world. Especially..." He gazed smugly from Sarah to Emmie and back. "... since I'm heading off to live in a haunted house of my own."

"What?" Sarah's mouth dropped open.

"I knew you were up to something." Emmie scowled playfully.

He nodded again. "I *am* up to something. I rented a cursed house."

"You already have an apartment, right? Did you get kicked out?"

He scoffed. "Kicked out? Me? No, actually my lease was up, so I was going to move somewhere else, anyway. And why not a place like, say, Caine House in Lake Eden? It was for rent, and I'm on my way over there to sign the lease now. You've heard of Caine House, right?"

Emmie sobered up at the mention of the house. "I've heard stories, yes. And you're worried about Alice still, but you would rent a place on purpose that you know is swarming with paranormal activity?"

"That's exactly the reason. Sarah moved into this place knowing that it's haunted, didn't she?"

"Sarah's situation is a little different from yours."

"Alice doesn't haunt us," Sarah said. "She's more like a roommate now."

"Well, this is my chance to immerse myself in everything I've been researching. When will I get another chance to live in a haunted house for an extended period?"

"How long did you rent it for?"

"I asked for a three-month lease because I figured I'd get plenty of data by then, but the owner insisted I sign for at least six months. I can always move out early if things get too bad."

Emmie stared at him for a moment, not hiding her skepticism. "Maybe the ghosts will have you running for your life after the first night."

Finn slowly formed a smile. "But that's what I was going to ask—if you two wouldn't mind stopping by after I move in, just for a day or so, you know, to get your insights on the situation. How does that sound?"

Emmie and Sarah looked at each other. Sarah rolled her eyes, and Emmie nodded at her. "Yeah, like Sarah said, Psychics R Us."

"That's cute. You should trademark it," Finn said. "And exactly. It's not just for your beautiful eyes or lovely purple hair that I need you there."

"We can't go today," Emmie said, gesturing toward the box. "You've caught us in the middle of going through a lot of stuff."

He looked at the box curiously. "Oh? What kind of stuff?"

She stood and opened the box on the counter, pulling out a small object wrapped in a hand cloth from the top of the pile. She unfurled it and rolled her eyes. Just a thin, quarter-sized old rune stone with an odd symbol etched across its face. "Who would have guessed? A rune stone."

Finn and Sarah joined her at the counter as she turned the stone over in her hands. Emmie focused on the hole near the top of the stone, and the symbol reminded her of a bird. Maybe someone had used it as a necklace.

Finn peered over the edge of the box, then gazed at the rune stone. "It's kind of cool."

"Want it?" She held it out toward him. "My gift to you—add it to your collection. There's probably a hundred more like it in there."

He accepted it, but peered into the box again, and pointed to something inside. "What else do you have in there? What's the book?"

"Let's see." Emmie dug in again, this time grabbing a book. It was the size of a small Bible, well-worn and bound in brown leather with the title *Mots de la Mort*. She held it up toward Finn. "This?"

"Yes." Finn set the rune stone on the counter. "That looks interesting."

Emmie looked it over, then glanced inside the box again. A chill raced up her spine. "Oh."

"What's wrong?" Sarah asked.

"This is from the accident. Whatever was left in my parents' car after the crash." She leaned against the counter as Finn threw her a concerned glance. "John told me he put the box in the garage."

Approaching them, Sarah rested her hand on Emmie's shoulder. "Do you want me to carry it back out there?"

"No, it's okay. I'll go through the rest later."

Finn stared at the book now. "Sorry, I didn't know."

"None of us did. But..." She gazed at the book, then up to Finn. His eyes were so full of wonder, so she handed it to him.

"It's all in French," Finn said. "*Words of Death* is an intriguing title, don't you think?" He stopped on one page and started reading. "*Accordez-moi le pouvoir sur toute la terre et tout ce qui se trouve sous la terre afin que mes ennemis s'assoient à mes pieds. Leurs prières seront mon nom, ô divine...*"

"Stop." Emmie snatched the book from him. "You shouldn't

just start reading a book like this out loud!"

He raised his eyebrows. "You're right, sorry."

"What does it say?" Sarah asked.

"Something about giving me power over everything on earth..." Finn said.

Emmie shook her head and scoffed. "Yeah, you'd love that."

"... and under the earth," he added with a grimace.

"That, maybe not so much." She narrowed her eyes at him. "Or who knows?"

"You speak French too?" Sarah asked him.

"Just a little bit. High school French plus a girlfriend in Paris. A couple of times." He paused and met their eyes. "What? Quickest way to learn a language." Finn gently pried the book from Emmie's hands. "I would love to study it. Mind if I take it with me?"

Emmie hesitated, but relented. "I guess. If you swear not to read it out loud, Finn. Could be silly hocus pocus, but we just don't know."

"Trust *moi*." Finn looked at his watch. "Well, I was just stopping by to let you know about my new place and extend my invitation. I have to get back to the house and sign the papers. After I get settled in there and you finish up here, you can come and introduce me to the *other tenants*?"

He stepped toward the door, followed by Emmie and Sarah.

"I guess we can't just leave you there defenseless."

"Exactly."

"Just be careful and don't stir anything up." Emmie walked beside him. She already regretted lending him the book. "You never know the history of a house like that and what the spirits might be capable of."

Finn nodded in agreement and paused for a moment, glancing back at the living room. "Is she there now?"

Emmie looked for Alice, but didn't see her. "She's gone."

"Hmm." He turned and walked out the door. "Later."

After Finn left, Emmie returned to the kitchen with Sarah

and closed the top of the box. Just touching it, knowing that the things inside it had been with her parents when they died, connected her to them in a morbid way. What had they been doing? Where had they been going? She'd never asked anyone those questions before, but now she wanted to know. "I guess the time is coming when I should try to find out what happened to Mom and Dad."

"Doesn't John know?" Sarah asked.

Emmie shook her head. "No. He told me so at the funeral. They were speeding and just swerved off the road into a tree."

"Do you think you could ever—"

Emmie knew what Sarah was hesitating to ask and shook her head. "I can't. If I saw them even a moment..." She held back the rising pain in her chest. "You know, they died in Lake Eden, not far from the house Finn rented, but that's all I know. I've never wanted to go anywhere near there and now... Coincidence, right?"

Sarah stiffened and widened her eyes.

Emmie gave a small laugh and pretended to feel braver than she did. "Sorry to spook you. I'll think about it later, but I know you need to visit your grandmother, right?"

"Yes." Sarah's eyes filled with sadness, and she checked the time on her cellphone. "I should probably leave now."

"Would you like me to go with?"

"No, thank you. I might be there for a while. I'll be okay."

Sarah left a short time later, and Emmie stood next to the kitchen counter, crying, with Alice Hyde watching from across the room.

Finn had forgotten the rune stone on the counter, but he'd gotten a better present with the book, anyway. She pulled out her car keys and examined the rune stone again before slipping it onto her key chain. Finn was right; it *was* kind of cool. "A gift... to myself."

Emmie gazed at the box on the counter again. "Recovered."

Not quite yet.

3

Finn and the caretaker stood on the steps of the Caine House before going inside. The caretaker's outfit stood out sharply against his own. The man wore a finely tailored suit and tie, buttoned up to the top as if he'd just stepped out of an executive's conference room. His brown leather dress shoes were polished with no sign of wear and tear, and his thick, brown hair was slicked over to one side with not a single gray hair, despite the deep wrinkles that lined his joyless, old face. The man was all business.

The caretaker motioned to the clean masonry construction and pointed out its historical value. "You won't see many unique places like this in central Minnesota. Caine House has been on the cover of three magazines, and the subject of many articles."

"That's how I found it," said Finn, without adding anything about the careful online research.

"Good. Then you understand how important it is to keep this place in good condition throughout your stay. I'm assuming you appreciate that."

"I do. Such a fantastic house with such a lot of rich history."

Finn glimpsed the darkened interior through a window a few feet away. White, ornate curtains blocked most of the view, and an antique lamp sat on a wooden table just behind the glass. He eyed the front door and pressed his lips together to avoid asking questions... yet. The caretaker had taken his time getting from the car to the steps, but now he was pointing out details that had no bearing. Finn stepped toward the door.

The caretaker opened it slowly and stepped aside to let Finn go in first.

That's more like it.

Finn gasped after stepping through the entryway. The wood-work and antiques inside were far beyond his expectations. It was like going back in time, and he resisted the urge to express his excitement. He'd been careful not to mention anything about the experiments he intended to conduct, or the caretaker would have voided their rental agreement in a heartbeat.

"The check?" The caretaker looked at his pocket.

"Oh yes." Finn dug it out and passed it to him.

The man scrutinized it, then surrendered the key. "Now, to emphasize, this is a historical landmark. You'll hear a lot of the typical sounds you might expect from something of this age. The floors squeak and the walls groan, so I don't expect to receive phone calls complaining about such things."

Not like all your other tenants, probably. "Understood."

The caretaker continued, "The furnace needs to be updated, but you expressed that you'd be comfortable dealing with those types of things?"

"I'm sure I can handle it. I'm good at repairing things."

"Glad to hear it."

They walked through the living room, and the caretaker seemed to eye the walls and doors as if expecting a surprise. But something else caught Finn's attention—portraits of the same man everywhere. A large one dominated the wall in the main entrance area, and smaller ones filled the space between the windows. No mistaking that this was Victor Caine, and it was *his* home.

Noticing his interest, the caretaker gestured to one of the

portraits. "By the way, you shouldn't take down any of the portraits. They'd get damaged easily. This and the furniture are the reason your deposit was a little higher than what you might expect somewhere else."

"Yet the rent is curiously... affordable." Finn tilted his chin up and clasped his hands behind his back, mimicking the man as he walked beside him.

"It's a large house, true," the caretaker said. "But in a small town, without much traffic. It's not suitable for a family because it's old and full of precious antiques, plus it takes a special sort of tenant to accept the responsibilities that come with it." He motioned around. "As you see, the workmanship is exquisite."

Finn walked over to the stairs and gripped the oak handrail. Solid as a rock. The stairs turned right halfway up at a landing, overshadowed by a large ornate window. "Yes, nothing ordinary about this house. Why didn't the owners take all the special antiques before renting it out?"

Clearing his throat and pursing his lips, the caretaker finally said, "I can't speak for Mr. Goodson and his family, but as a wealthy man, I'm sure he has plenty of household items without the need for more clutter in his home, and maybe doesn't care for this style?"

It made sense. Finn had done the research on Mr. Goodson previously, as the Caine family's only living descendent, coming from Victor's mother's side, as the founder of Lake Eden hadn't had children. A great-grandcousin twice removed, who had inherited the house and the family fortune after selling off Caine Industries. Mr. Goodson was wealthy, true, and probably couldn't sell the house for any amount of money, as rumors of it being haunted had persisted for over a hundred years. That didn't stop some brave or clueless souls from renting it every so often, but those rentals had never lasted very long. Maybe Mr. Goodson was hoping for someone who played nice with the spirits to buy the house, and in the meantime, the occasional tenants would help keep the pipes from rusting and the rats from taking over. At least, Finn hoped so. He would definitely take ghosts over rats any day.

Finn nodded. "Which room was Victor's?"

"Let me take you there."

Detailed, gaudy, red and white wallpaper covered most of the walls. Lots of old framed photos lined the stairs. Too many to count. Three old lamps protruding up from the balcony overhead lit the way. A massive, colorful mural occupied the space above eye level near the ceiling, featuring an idealistic country setting with fields, animals, forests, and a lake devoid of any human figures.

Finn gestured to it. "That's Lake Eden?"

The caretaker glanced up without pausing. "Yes, we assume so. As I mentioned previously, all the bedrooms are furnished. The owner did this to prevent tenants from dragging their furniture and beds up and down the stairs. If you have your own furniture, I ask that you store it out in the provided garage or discard it. Unless you rent for a much longer time, I doubt you'll need it."

"I can put my stuff in the garage. Is that what most other tenants have done?" *To run away faster?*

The caretaker didn't answer.

Along the hallway at the top of the stairs, several doors sat wide open, and the sunlight beamed in through the open windows at the far end of the hallway. It actually looked pleasant.

"Mr. Caine's bedroom is at the end of the hall." The caretaker continued walking. "I'm guessing that's where you'll be staying, but you're free to pick any of them. You can have guests stay with you, but not subtenants, and I won't tolerate any parties at the house."

"Not fond of parties."

"Good."

The caretaker motioned to the open door in the hallway next to Victor's room. "I'm afraid there's only one bathroom upstairs, as was the case for most houses back then. It wasn't common to have four or five bathrooms like they do nowadays. If you don't have a lot of guests, it shouldn't be a problem."

"As long as the toilet works." Finn grinned.

Without waiting for Finn to explore the other rooms, the caretaker circled back toward the stairs again. The house echoed with their footsteps as they descended.

Stepping onto the main floor again, they reached the kitchen and found two doors near the back side of the house. One door led out into the backyard and the other revealed stairs to the basement.

The caretaker flipped on the basement light. "Not much down there, except the furnace, cement walls and a few spiderwebs. The basement walls were originally just bare dirt, as was common back then, and we propped them up as best we could to prevent the foundation from sagging. But the stone construction of the house is solid. The masonry is top notch for its time."

"Like some English castle."

The caretaker eyed him. "Are you sure you aren't interested in signing a one-year lease? It's cheaper per month in the long run."

"Six months for now, thank you."

"Fine. Do you have any other questions for me?"

The floor squeaked as Finn stepped over to a window and turned back. After he stopped, something thudded against the floorboards beneath them.

"That would be the furnace I was referring to," the caretaker said.

The moment had come. Finn took a dramatic hand to his chest. "Uff da. For a second, I thought it might be a ghost!"

The caretaker scowled and met Finn's eyes. "That's absurd."

Oh, you are trying to repress me, and I haven't even started? "Maybe I just read too many stories."

"You can ignore all the silly stories and rumors. Rest assured, you'll be seeing none of that here. There's no reason to entertain tales of haunted nonsense. Nobody died in the house and anything you've heard contrary to that is hogwash." The caretaker turned toward the kitchen. "All the cabinetry is from the early 1900s, original to the house, but the owners renovated some things over the years. I mentioned the furnace earlier. It's about thirty years old, but it works just fine. And we have updated all the appliances within the last five years."

Finn followed him. "Victor Caine didn't die in this house? I think I read—"

"Everyone died at home at that time," the man said curtly. "That's nothing to worry about. Mr. Caine founded this town. Have you visited the monument over his grave in the cemetery about a mile down the road?"

"I haven't stopped by yet."

"You should. And I advise you to visit the memorial at City Hall, which gives a more comprehensive description of his achievements. The more you know about him and the impact he had on this town, the more you will appreciate living here."

"I also read accounts of previous tenants just running away. What happened?"

The caretaker shook his head, and his face reddened. "A few unreliable sources say crazy things like that. People believe what they want to believe rather than do their research and examine the truth. It's just an old house *without* scandals or murders or suicides. Nothing like that happened here."

"No murders, no suicides, huh?"

"None of that. Go to the county courthouse and check the records if you'd like. Nothing exists to back up the superstitious claims." He crossed his arms over his chest, wrinkling his immaculate suit. "Any further questions of relevance?"

"Not that I can think of right now."

"Right, then all I ask is that you treat this home with respect."

"Sure."

After throwing Finn a doubtful glance, the caretaker walked

to the front door without further eye contact, and they shook hands one last time before they parted.

When the door closed, leaving Finn surrounded only by silence and emptiness, a chill of excitement surged through his chest. He wanted to run out to his car at that moment and grab all his equipment, but he would need to wait until the caretaker had driven away.

He glanced around with a grin. An entire haunted house all to himself. A six-month-long research vacation without needing to bother anyone or worry that he might get kicked out or arrested. A ghost hunter's paradise... as long as the caretaker was wrong about the stories.

Finn rubbed his hands together. Might as well get things started.

❦ 4 ❧

Her grandmother wasn't in the hospital where Sarah worked, but the rooms and smells and bustling urgency were the same. The hospice area looked no different from any other part of the hospital, but it was the place they brought patients who were expected to die. Half of them passed away within three weeks of entering.

Sarah hesitated before walking into her grandmother's hospital room. Her previous visit a few days earlier had brought her to tears, and she wanted to show her strength this time, lift her grandmother's spirit rather than be weighed down by the horrible event that had transformed the once lively old woman into a struggling, partially paralyzed stroke victim.

She squeezed the vase of roses in her hands and felt the dampness of her palms on the glass surface. *Why am I so nervous this time?* She should be used to it by now, having approached so many other patients in the same dire situation, but now it was different. It was *her* grandmother in there—Grandma Elizabeth —and everything lovely she offered the world was behind the curtain hanging between them, trapped in that shell of an old woman.

While she was standing at the edge of the door, the doctor

approached her with a pleasant smile and a clipboard in his hand. Dr. Forrester. Sarah recognized him from the last visit.

He moved in beside her. "Hello again."

She forced a smile. "How is she?"

He stepped away and gestured for her to follow him. They walked a few steps down the hallway before he turned to her and lowered the clipboard with a compassionate stare. "I'm afraid she's not getting better. I'm not sure she'll survive much longer in this condition. It could be months, or it could be days."

Losing her smile, she glanced at the floor. "I was hoping she'd be able to talk better by now."

"It's important to keep expectations low at this point. The stroke injured a large section of her brain."

Sarah's body grew cold. She knew from experience what the next steps in her grandmother's care would be. Hospice was never a good sign, but now the doctor's eyes had that *look*. The *knowing* that things wouldn't turn out in the patient's favor while not wanting to destroy her last bit of hope.

Still, she asked, "Do you think she will come out of it?"

The doctor shrugged. "It's hard to say."

No, she won't. "I was hoping she might wake up, even for a short time, just long enough to say goodbye."

He gently put his hand on her shoulder. "Sometimes they come back, but the pain medication makes her drowsy."

"Morphine?"

"Yes." He tilted his head, as if pondering the possibilities. "We'll take good care of her."

No, that was never good. Her grandmother was in a bad place. "Thank you, Dr. Forrester."

Morphine would keep her grandmother in bed and comfortable, but with little chance that she would talk coherently, even with her eyes wide open. She wanted comfort for her grandmother, but she didn't want to see her succumb to the stroke without a fight.

"You can try talking to her now," Dr. Forrester said. "She

might wake up, but I'm not sure she'll respond. Her health has deteriorated since you were last here."

"Thank you. I'm going in there."

The doctor nodded. "Yes, I'm sure she'd appreciate it."

Sarah forced a smile, then walked into her grandmother's room. The old woman was lying almost in the same position as during their last visit, but now she faced the window. Sarah wanted to rip away all the tubes and devices, sit her up, and walk her out of there. A hospital bed was no place for a woman so full of wisdom and strength.

Her grandmother's face was a little more pale, her cheeks more gaunt, and her eyes cracked open as Sarah stepped across the room with the roses. Forming a weak smile, her grandmother's hand twitched as she struggled to speak, but only a single word came out, "Love."

"I wanted to bring something to cheer you up, Grandma."

Her grandmother's face was red and strained, her lips tight on one side as if she were pulling them to free a piece of food from her teeth. She moaned and gestured with one finger for Sarah to come closer.

Sarah carefully moved her cheek alongside her grandmother's face. Maybe she would give her a kiss.

Instead, her grandmother turned and whispered into her ear, "Garden."

Sarah backed away and looked into her grandmother's eyes. All those years of being so close to her now came back, and she understood what her grandmother was asking her perfectly. *The garden.* Her grandmother always talked about heaven as a garden, and how one day they would share it together, but it still came as a surprise to hear her say the word. *Maybe she really has meant for me to take her to the hospital garden outside?*

"You want me to take you outside?" Sarah asked.

Almost imperceptibly, her grandmother shook her head.

Sarah had understood correctly, but she stiffened. "I can't."

Now her grandmother cringed as if a flare of pain had shot through her. Her grandmother's strong emotions filled Sarah, almost unbearable pain at that distance, and she wanted to back away.

Sarah held her grandmother's hand, watching the old woman's eyes open and close drearily, until her grandmother silently mouthed the same word. Garden. "I don't want you to go, Grandma. If I release you like the others, I don't know if I can live with that. It's not the same."

Her grandmother smiled and closed her eyes, her mouth still softly opening and closing now without forming any particular word. But she didn't need words—it was understood. She was encouraging Sarah to do the right thing.

Sarah's hands shook as she stood up and stared down at her grandmother's face. She wanted so much for this lovely woman to come alive and go back home where they could spend another afternoon talking about quilting and life experiences, and laugh about all the crazy things they'd been through. Sarah wanted it all back the way it was, and she stood there knowing it could all be over in minutes.

Sarah sensed her grandmother's spirit in the room, a beacon of light and love that surrounded them like a cocoon. It wouldn't be difficult from a practical point of view to give her spirit a little push, help her on her way.

Tears formed in Sarah's eyes and dripped down her cheeks. This would be the last moment with her grandmother, but... no. She held on and didn't let go. No, she wouldn't be the one to separate them forever. She couldn't.

She let go of her grandmother's hand, placing it gently beside the bed, and stepped back. "I'm sorry, Grandma."

Turning, she left the room, grabbing a chair in the hallway just outside the door as tears still streamed down her cheeks. She wiped her eyes with the back of her hand. Nurses passed by, rushing to do their jobs just as she had done so many times while family members sat crying outside her patient's room. She stared at the floor. She would leave when she stopped crying.

"Sarah?"

Sarah looked up and her mother was standing over her, looking down with sorrowful eyes. "Did you see your grandma yet?"

Her mother always had a way of showing up at the right time. They'd always had a special sort of connection between them. And it was something about the way her mother's earthy brown eyes gazed down on her that just made everything instantly feel better. She had a warm presence, so full of love.

She was wearing her dental hygienist's work uniform now. Most likely, she had stopped by the hospital on her way home after getting a *hunch* that Sarah was there. Her mother's brown curly hair was more frazzled than normal, but in the sterile light of the hospital, she looked like an angel.

Sarah nodded.

Her mother sat down next to her and pulled her in closer. "It'll be okay. What time did you get here?"

"Fifteen minutes ago."

"How is she doing?"

"Awful."

Her mom rocked her a few times. "We'll get through it."

"I don't want her to suffer. I'm a nurse, Mom, I'm supposed to help people, but I can't help her."

Her mom nudged her, glancing down the hall. "Let's take a walk."

Sarah stood up with her and walked down the hallway. They didn't speak until they entered the break room. A television blared in the corner, but the room was empty. Her mother led her over to the farthest table and took her hand after they sat down.

"You've got a beautiful heart, Sarah," her mom said. "Your dad and I were so happy when you decided to be a nurse, and your grandmother was even more thrilled than I was. I know you want to save her, but the doctors are doing everything they can."

"Grandma wants to leave, Mom."

A confused look passed over her mom's face. "What do you mean?"

"She wants to die. She told me. And she said that because she knows I can help her."

"How?"

Sarah hesitated. "I know you don't believe in all that psychic stuff..."

Her mom was silent.

"... but Grandma really could heal others. That's why I wanted to be a nurse in the first place, to be like her. And I *am* like her, in a way, but it's hard to explain. I can feel the emotions of those around me with such clarity, it's so overwhelming sometimes that I can't handle it. Now I feel Grandma's pain and her desire to pass on. I can help her do that, I can lift her spirit and send her on her way, but... not for Grandma. I don't want her to go."

Her mom nodded. "Your grandma was always doing stuff like that throughout her life, and I had a hard time believing it until you came along and I saw some of the same qualities in you. She is right that you are special. And I always noticed that you two had a deep connection. I guess the gift you share skipped a generation with me—but even though I don't understand it, I think you should do what's right."

"I can feel her suffering now." Sarah held back more tears.

"Then we should respect her decision and whatever she needs you to do, I accept that."

Sarah nodded and stood up. "I don't want her to leave."

Her mom stood with her. "It's not for us to decide. The world needs more compassion, Sarah, and I know you're an expert at that."

They walked back into the hospice area of the hospital and back into her grandmother's room. A group of nurses shouted in the hallway, along the way, breaking the reverence of the moment. Not the ideal scenario for such a sacred occasion.

They stood side by side next to her grandmother, and Sarah lifted the old woman's bent hand.

Sarah's mom placed her hand on Sarah's, so all three touched each other. "Everything will be all right."

Sarah made peace with herself and looked into her grandmother's closed eyes. "Okay, Grandma. It's time to go. I love you."

"I love you too," her mother said beside her.

Sarah waited until her grandmother's breathing slowed before bending down and kissing her forehead. She put her other hand on her grandmother's shoulder.

Her grandmother cringed and shuddered for a moment as if stung by a needle. The emotional pain passing through her grandmother grew, but within that pain was a surge of excitement too. She was getting revved up to go.

The sensations of light and warmth filled Sarah and passed through her to her grandmother, and then a joyous sensation of love filled the room as her grandmother separated from her body and rose. A few seconds later, the familiar hospital alarms went off, and the staff rushed into the room, wondering what had happened. Sarah and her mom stepped back as the hospital staff did their jobs.

"She has a Do Not Resuscitate order," Sarah's mom reminded them.

"Yes, thank you," a nurse responded.

Dr. Forrester rushed in a minute later and after determining she had passed on, they all stopped their work.

Serenity filled the room and Sarah stared at her grandmother's face. *Such peace.* She took that image and the connection of love she'd shared with her grandmother with her as she walked out of the room and headed back to her car with her mom. Holding back her tears, she questioned her actions, but kept it to herself. Had she *really* done the right thing? If so, then why was it so painful? Her body and mind were numb. This wound would take a long time to heal.

She gave her mom a hug, and they parted as she climbed into the driver's seat of her car again. She cried for an hour before driving away.

It took Finn almost two hours to unpack his car and bring everything inside the house, not because he had so many things to carry in, but because some additional element of the house distracted him with each trip. The carved stonework on the exterior, the intricate layers of the coffered ceilings, the scratched wood floors, the antique window locks, and the hand-carved oak mantle outlining the fireplace. And despite the house's age, the owners and previous tenants had taken good care of it.

They could have used it as a museum, although only the larger, more permanent items remained, probably because nobody could get them out of the house without destroying it.

Aside from the bulky furniture, they hadn't bothered to remove the most striking feature facing visitors after walking through the front door. Prominent relics of the house's history—the six oil paintings of Mr. Caine, which reminded everyone at every turn that this was his house, and you were just a guest.

The largest portrait, even larger than the one in the entrance, hung along the side wall in the living room. The frame's design gave the appearance that Mr. Caine had constructed the wall just for showing off this single grand image, but every painting showed the man in a different, harrowing situation. In one he brandished a rifle during a buffalo hunt, and in another he wore a military uniform complete with medals and the American flag waving prominently in the background. A smaller painting showed him joined by five other armed men, all of them standing next to him proudly, as if they had just won a great battle. Each face was stern and cold—the norm back then. Nobody smiled for anything.

The entryway, living room, and the side foyer were roughly the same size as Finn's entire apartment with plenty of space to explore. How many rooms did the caretaker say the place had? He had missed that detail, probably lulled by the man droning on and on, and by Finn's own happiness at standing in an alleged goldmine of paranormal activity. It didn't matter, anyway. It was a fortress, maybe four times larger than an average house.

Finn set up one camera on a tripod in the living room, although he would position it later. He just wanted to get *something* up and ready to capture whatever surprises lay in store for him. He set up a few other devices before unpacking his clothes or stopping to eat. Priorities. Even with six months of research ahead of him, he intended to record as much as possible. He didn't want to miss even a minute.

Carrying a night vision camera, he made a slow tour through the house, moving further into the corners and closets the caretaker had ignored or avoided. Finn opened every door and peeked behind every piece of furniture in search of hidden doors or clues that might reveal a mystery. In a few drawers he found keys, some old and large, and he pocketed them all in case any rooms were locked.

Without knowing the full background of the house, he could only rely on the stories he'd read on the Internet, some of them from former tenants who had complained of slamming doors and nighttime footsteps along with plenty of creeping shadows. Generic characteristics for a haunted house. But he intended to stir up as much activity as he could while he was there.

A door squeaked in the next room near the kitchen.

"Not yet, Mr. Caine," Finn said. "I haven't got all my equipment ready."

A couple more hours, maybe three, and he would have all the main equipment recording, and the following day he planned to examine the data from the previous night. He'd keep up that cycle for as long as he could, either until he discovered something or it became too much to handle. He'd even purchased two more sets of devices just for the special occasion.

No matter the caretaker didn't believe that the house was haunted—the stories Finn had found online were detailed enough to stir his imagination. Maybe his investment would be a bust, but the opportunity was just too good to resist.

Walking through the hallway upstairs, he stopped at each bedroom, holding his digital video camera out at chest level and stopping at a few of the other paintings along the way. One showed armed men battling Native Americans in an open field near a lake, which resembled Lake Eden. Another was a photo of an old building with the words Caine Industries written across a large pane of glass in the front. At the bottom, the date: 1901.

After getting settled in, Finn planned to visit the Victor Caine Memorial in front of City Hall in town and also the Monument to the Innocents near Caine Industries, marking where over fifty original settlers had been massacred. If he was lucky, he'd find out about a few previous tenants of Caine House. Someone in town might share inside information not readily available online. He'd tried to get the name of a previous tenant for "reference" purposes when he first asked about the place, but the caretaker had refused to give him any information, citing "privacy issues." *Right.*

Finn walked into one of the guest rooms and stared out the window toward the fields beyond the edge of the property. A stream divided the Caine House lawn from a sprawling cornfield, but toward the far-left side of the lawn, at the edge of the stream, stood a small stone structure with a door but no windows. It was ordinary in its construction, unlike everything else around the house, and the caretaker hadn't mentioned it during the tour.

Probably just full of lawn equipment. But the door was small, not practical for that purpose. *Maybe an old well or guest house?*

Another strange feature of Mr. Caine's house.

Still carrying the video camera with him, Finn walked back downstairs and around the house to the backyard. He strolled across the freshly cut grass to the odd structure, examining its construction from a distance. With the stream nearby, maybe it had been a deluxe outhouse?

Arriving at the door, he studied its thick metal frame and un-Caine-like door handle. It resembled a compact prison more than a guest house. *Even a better reason to explore it.* There was a thick modern-day padlock around the latch. Finn pulled out the keys the caretaker had given him and tried both on the padlock. Neither worked.

"I guess I won't be going in there. Unless..." He walked around to the back of the structure. No windows at all.

He touched his pocket. The keys he had found earlier in the drawers pressed against his fingers. He dug them out and began trying the ones that would fit in the padlock. It finally clicked open at the third key, and the metal door squeaked as he pulled it back and peered inside.

Hot, stale air floated out and the afternoon sunlight revealed that the structure was almost empty. Almost. In the center sat a cement slab about two feet high, three feet wide, and seven feet long. An ornate black iron cross rose from the head of the slab.

A crypt?

The caretaker had denied that anyone had died on the property, but he couldn't take anything the caretaker said at face value—renting a haunted house was a tough sell. Even the information he'd uncovered on the Internet about Victor Caine showed a picture of his grave at the town cemetery, so maybe this was a family member? Finn would definitely need to research more information about it.

He glanced back toward the house before stepping into the crypt and located Victor Caine's bedroom window. Just darkness and the reflection of cloudy skies. But he had a strange sensation that someone was watching him. "I'm going in for a *look*."

Moving cautiously inside, he used his cellphone in flashlight mode to light the area with one hand and filmed it with the other. Plenty of cobwebs and dust. He moved across the crypt to the head of the slab and studied the details of the fancy iron cross. No name, but there was an inscription running across both arms. *La mort a fermé ses yeux. Que votre main ne le réveille pas.*

Death has closed these eyes. May your hand not awake him. *Or her?* It could be either in French.

This was better than the house as the ideal place to record first. A gravesite with an exotic cross, a message, and nobody to question him. *Perfect.*

Hurrying back into the house, he was retrieving a few devices when his eyes fell on the book he had taken from Emmie.

Could it help clear up anything? He opened it and by leafing through the index he found the sentence on the cross right away under the heading, *"Le doux baiser du sommeil."* This meant something like the sweet kiss of sleep.

"Well, my friend, you're coming with." He closed the book and stuck it inside his waistband as he picked up the devices.

At the structure, he set up them up to record outside and within. He took a device he had modified, combining the EMF and light and sound to produce wave pulses that could then be recorded and analyzed as they struck the surrounding surfaces using some specialized software he had run across on the Internet. He could focus his modified device on a wide range of frequencies so that the pulses produced an image like sonar within the software. The intention was to develop a new way to detect the unseen.

He called this Frankenstein device made from assorted electronics fused into one piece the size of a shoebox the "Beast." Now he attached it to the top of another tripod. Switching it on and using the light from his cell phone, he took the French book from his waist and scanned through it for any clues as to the meaning of the inscription on the cross. The reference was about seventy pages in. Below it was another longer line of French text, but those words were a bit more complicated to translate. He was aware that his accent was often better than his comprehension—as a couple of Parisians had pointed out rather nastily; but he remembered not to read the words aloud, as Emmie had insisted. All he understood was that *Les Mots de la Mort* was what the title announced—a book dealing with death or funeral rites.

He abandoned the book in favor of studying the cross more closely. The base was not cemented but screwed into the slab. That seemed unusual enough to warrant him giving the whole cross a spin; he would lift it off the base a bit to examine it. The iron and the handiwork on it might give him an idea of the age of the artifact and therefore of the grave.

Was it old metal work, going back to Victor's time, or more recent?

The cross seemed at first unwilling to budge. He had to grasp it with both hands and push with all his strength to make it move an inch, but after a lot of straining, groaning, and cursing, he managed finally to turn it. He had to stop and rest, panting a bit, but after that first success, it moved more easily. A lubricant spray might have helped, but he hadn't brought any with. As the cross rose, showing the corkscrew shape at the bottom, Finn could tell it was definitely not new. The iron work was more than a century old. This was created in another kind of industry, not mass produced.

What the hell are you doing?

His own question stopped him when the cross was almost out of the hole. How stupid would he have to be to pull that out completely before he had time to research more? He'd learned long ago to respect tombs and graves, as it ought to be ingrained in anyone who studied the paranormal, so what was he doing?

Finn hesitated as he reflected. But before he started to screw the large cross back into place, the base glowed yellow and white for a moment before it burst into the air, smashing into the stone ceiling then crashing down again to the floor. The clanging of the iron when it hit the stone was deafening in that tiny space. At the same time, a flash of white light burst through the room, and a force like someone shoving him aside knocked him to the ground. The book was knocked from the slab as well, and a low moan filled the air before the door to the structure slammed shut.

Panic swelled as Finn's heartbeat raced, and he staggered to his feet. He jumped toward the door, thrusting it outward with all his strength, but it opened again without much effort.

He gasped in a deep breath and stumbled outside, looking back in to find his cellphone lighting the walls from the floor of the crypt.

What the hell had just happened?

The cross.

He couldn't have screwed it back in place if he'd wanted. The corkscrew shape was destroyed at the bottom, as if it had melted. He'd broken the cross, but how?

Had someone booby-trapped it? That must be it. A little bit of gunpowder tucked within the shaft of the cross. An explosive set to scare the crap out of anyone who messed with the grave, or even blow off the intruder's hand as mentioned in the inscription.

Approaching the doorway again, he stared inside and spoke to whoever they might have buried in there, and, who knew, piping mad at him. "I'm very sorry. I'll fix it."

A gust of wind stirred the hair behind his ears, and he glanced back outside. The same wind that had knocked him backwards?

✺ 6 ✺

The sense of wrongdoing passed as Finn analyzed the data he'd recorded in the crypt for an hour. He discovered his Beast hadn't worked as expected. Not only had it recorded unusable data, but even his reliable digital video camera only revealed a flash of white light that washed out all the details, followed by a solid black screen for several seconds before it faded back to the original image. Disappointing result, but an interesting occurrence he would have to follow up on.

My first ghost?

He'd converted a guest room upstairs into his new office. It only consisted of a couple of card tables and folding chairs for now, but it worked well enough as a place for his research. After discovering the data had been a total loss, a faint, garbled conversation downstairs caught his attention. The voices shouted, indistinct and distant, as if two men were finding their way up from the basement in the dark. He'd brought along his TV but didn't remember turning it on. Had he left on a piece of equipment? A video advertisement playing in the background on his laptop? But he didn't remember turning that on either. Maybe the caretaker had come back to snoop on him.

Finn walked downstairs and circled around to the area

directly beneath the makeshift office where he'd been working. No sign of anyone inside the house, but he called out anyway. "Hello? Is someone here?"

Except for the walls creaking as the wind picked up outside, there was only silence.

A nearby door attracted his attention. He opened it but was disappointed to discover an empty closet. Lots of space in that house, which Victor must have filled at one time with a hoard of possessions judging by the portraits on the walls. Another door near the kitchen opened to an extra pantry lined with empty shelves.

Exploring a hallway leading toward the back of the house, Finn stepped into a small room with two windows and a small desk. Another portrait of Victor hung on one wall beside a door. *Freaking narcissist.* Finn tried to open it, but it was locked. His eyes narrowed, and he grinned. Nothing would stop him from exploring every inch of that house. *I intend to get my money's worth, Mr. Caine.*

The bronze and glass doorknob jiggled in his grip, and he pulled a little harder, just in case the door was only jammed. Glancing around the room for ledges where he might find a key strategically placed for such an occasion, he gave up and bent down, peering into the forbidden room through the keyhole. A window just beyond his view flooded the room with daylight. A massive secretary's desk sat against the far wall with dozens of drawers and small doors. Lots of places to hide things and then forget about them. But how to get in there?

He touched the keys in his pocket. One of them *had* to work. He pulled them out and tried each one with no luck. Groaning as he slipped them back into his pocket, he shook the door handle harder now, as if a spirit might have pity on him and reward his failed attempts by unlocking the door. No, he would need to find another way in. It wouldn't be too difficult to climb in through the window from the outside, as long as it wasn't locked. Not ideal, but an option.

He peeked in through the keyhole, straining to get a better view of the room, until a shadow on the other side passed over the hole. He jumped back with his heart racing and focused on the light coming through under the door. No sounds, no movements, no shadows now. But he stood still and held his breath.

Silence filled the house.

Someone knocked at the front door, and he shuddered. "Dammit." Maybe the voices had been the caretaker. He walked through the house, and the visitor pounded again before he could answer. "I hear you."

Finn opened the door and faced a forty-something couple. They were giddy to meet him, both with wide smiles, and Finn expected a pitch to join a local congregation at any moment. The man's long brown hair was flying loose in the wind before he tamed it with his fingers and grinned. The woman stood with her arms folded over her chest.

"Sorry to interrupt you," the man said, "but we noticed someone moving in yesterday."

Finn braced himself for the solicitation. "That's me."

"I'm Laura, and this is my husband, Paul." The woman craned her neck, staring over Finn's shoulder inside the house as if expecting someone else to appear. "Are you here all alone?"

"Yes."

Her eyes widened, but Paul smiled politely. "We just saw some cars over here yesterday, and we wanted to say hi."

Finn nodded once. "Hi. You live around here?"

Paul gestured to his left. "Not too far down the road."

"You think it's a problem to be alone here?" Finn made his smile friendly and nonchalant.

"Well, it's been here more than a century," Paul said. "Lots of history, you know. Why, have you run into anything strange?"

The shadow behind the locked door and the muffled voices came to mind. "Nothing too strange."

"Are you planning to rent it a while?" Laura asked.

"I signed a six-month lease."

The man gave a low whistle. "That's a long time."

"Not normally for a rental, so I'm assuming you're talking about the rumors of ghosts."

"Yes." Laura glanced at Paul. "I think no one here would be caught dead spending a single night in this place."

Finn looked behind him. "I'm not too concerned. Just the usual noises—like you said, it's an old house. I'll let you know if any of the rumors are true."

Paul still craned his neck to look into the living room. "Cameras, huh? Are you planning to record the... noises?"

Finn shrugged. "Whatever I can."

"So you're a ghost hunter?"

Finn scoffed. "Do people like that really exist?"

Apparently not fooled, Laura pulled on her husband's arm. "Tell him about the Andersons."

Paul cleared his throat. "We met them on their way out of town a few years ago. They were in a panic then. One of the kids kept screaming about a scary man pulling her out of the bed and almost dragging her down the stairs. They left behind a bunch of stuff when they took off, didn't even bother to empty the drawers or anything, I heard. I guess the caretaker keeps the stuff that people leave behind, but that's the way it goes with this place."

"Do you know where the Andersons moved to?"

"No, but I'm sure it was as far away as they could get."

"And what ghosts do the town people think are here, then?"

Laura swallowed, staring over Finn's shoulder again.

The portrait.

"Victor? Really?" Finn asked. "I thought he was the hero of Lake Eden?"

An awkward moment of silence passed between them, which Paul filled by saying, as he took his wife's hand, "Well, you know. Stories passed down, but no one really knows anything."

Laura seemed to disagree, but they were already moving

backwards. "Well, we just wanted to introduce ourselves and welcome you to Lake Eden."

Finn nodded as they waved and headed off down the driveway.

He waited until the couple moved out of sight before grabbing his car keys and heading out the door. The couple's concern and their tale of the Anderson family intrigued him, and it was time to do a little research locally and find out what he could about the house and its past.

He'd spotted the memorial outside the City Hall as he came through town. Victor's statue was prominently displayed in the courtyard. That would be his first stop, and then he would pay a visit to another memorial near Caine Industries, the Monument to the Innocents.

He drove back toward town, winding along gravel roads before passing the cemetery on his left, at the edge of the main road. He would make a stop there too, but it would need to wait for another day.

Turning onto the main road, he followed it through town toward where he had seen the Victor Caine Memorial earlier. Within a few minutes, he pulled into the parking lot for City Hall. The statue of Mr. Caine stood almost defiantly on its pedestal in the front courtyard. A few police cars passed nearby, and Finn instinctively checked what he'd worn that day. Certain shirts and attire attracted law enforcement more than others, but he wasn't researching ghosts with handfuls of devices in the cemetery this time. He was just a resident now—no cause for alarm.

He climbed out of his car and walked over to the statue, staring up at the man; it seemed like he'd done a lot of that since arriving. It was similar to the portraits in the house, with the same glaring eyes, but the statue's intricate details and stance gave him an air of prestige, and now he wasn't just a photograph, or a news article, or a fine painting—Victor had lived and breathed and *thrived* in Lake Eden. If they'd intended to make him look larger than life, they had succeeded.

An inscription along the base of the statue revealed a little information about the man: Victor Caine, founder of Lake Eden, had defeated a band of thirty-two Sioux after they attacked and massacred fifty-seven innocent settlers—men, women, and children—along the shores of Lake Eden in 1898.

No more information than that on the plaque, so Finn headed to the front door of City Hall. Maybe someone inside would have more information.

A small elderly woman at a desk just inside the door intercepted him. "Can I help you?"

"Yes, maybe. I'm seeking more information about Victor Caine."

"You've come to the right place." The woman gestured to one side of the hallway a little further inside. "You can read the plaques on the wall there. They recount what happened back then." Her phone rang, and she picked it up before Finn could ask anything else.

Finn walked over to the plaques and started going through each one, taking pictures of a few—better than trying to remember it all. With each successive bit of information, he pieced together the tragic events that had given rise to Victor Caine's legacy.

Victor had not only founded the town, but Caine Industries. He'd built his business on the site of the massacre next to Lake Eden in defiance of the Native American resistance. Several photos showed Victor with five associates who had helped him avenge the death of the settlers, together with a posse of lawmen from the state. Victor's success led to dozens of Sioux tribesmen being killed in battle, but the attacks ceased, and the town quickly prospered under his stewardship.

After Finn finished reading, he walked back over to the old woman at the front desk. She looked up from the book she was reading, a romance.

"Do you know how he died?"

"It's listed in the city records as dysentery."

Finn cringed. "That doesn't sound like a... noble way to check out. At least not for a man of his stature."

She made a face as repressive as the caretaker's. "I'm sure even the greatest men don't choose the way they die. Death is a nasty thing, in most cases."

Her arched eyebrow told him that she wouldn't accept a joke well, and would not even engage in gossip. And he had thought people in small towns did nothing else. The great founder and hero was not to be mentioned lightly, it seemed.

Finn left City Hall and headed over to see the Monument to the Innocents by the lake, not far away.

The monument was at the edge of a park, shrouded by pine trees, but not much else. Not a particularly inviting area to visit. A single family was gathered around one of the picnic tables with an RV parked nearby. Beside the park sprawled Caine Industries, a patchwork of old red brick with a modern glass entryway.

Finn stepped over to the granite monument, which stood about four feet tall above a three-foot-high base. An inscription read:

This monument commemorates the life and courage of fifty-seven settlers, attacked and killed in 1896. Beneath these trees lie all the innocent souls within a single grave.

No other information was given. The plaque looked fairly new, and Finn assumed the mention of the Native Americans as the villains of the story had been removed in these more politically correct times, although the man who had engaged on a vendetta on behalf of the settlers was still the town hero.

Finn walked around the monument and weaved between the pine trees, finding another granite stone five feet wide and several feet long, this one lying flat against the ground. A simple epitaph was carved across the top, but the letters had filled in with dirt and had worn down. *Fifty-seven souls lie here.* Finn studied it. The same stone construction on this gravesite as at the crypt in the house. No surprise, seeing that they had most likely been manufactured at the same time.

Finn looked out at the complex of Caine Industries. What had happened to the spirits of those massacred by the Sioux? Were their souls still wandering the area, or had they found peace? Maybe Emmie would need to pay a visit to the place. If any of them were still there, she would certainly see at least the children who had died.

Before turning back to the car, Finn stepped around the flat granite monument and caught sight of something at the back edge of the park. A tall, thin, beige monument stood amidst a group of larger pine trees.

Walking over to it, he passed the family sitting at the picnic tables and pushed through the branches blocking a small clearing on the other side. A tower-like structure greeted him. Attached to the top was a single, black iron cross with the same size and design as the one in the crypt behind the Caine House.

Even from several feet away he could still read the inscription: *La mort a fermé ses yeux...*

Death had closed those eyes, and his hand must not awaken anyone...

7

Finn dangled his legs over the edge of an open grave. A shovel handle lay across his lap and a pile of black dirt sat next to him on the floor of the crypt. The grave's cement cover sat several feet away, and a simple, rotting pine casket lay wide open beside it, flipped over on its side. No sign of the corpse.

His brother Neil sat across from him, also with legs dangling over the edge. Neil's heels knocked back against the dirt wall as he flipped through the pages of *Mots de la Mort,* the occult book.

Neil looked up and grinned at Finn. "This is an interesting book."

"It's not a novel, Neil." But he knew his brother was joking; he had always played the joker, even more than Finn.

"No wonder you're so smart." Neil flipped through a few more pages. "Lots of good stuff in here. Read some of it to me." He leaned forward and stretched out the book toward Finn.

Finn didn't accept it. "I can't read that."

His brother laughed. "I can't read it either." Neil tossed the book to the side and looked down into the dark hole between them. "What do you plan to do now?"

"I guess I'll cover it back up." Finn gripped the handle of the shovel.

"Hold on there. There's nothing down there to bury. You let it out, remember?"

Finn almost gasped. "What did I let out?"

"That." Neil gestured to someone standing in the darkened corner of the crypt. The silhouette of a body wavered as Finn focused on the details of the face. All just a shadowy blur. A chill flashed through him. It was watching him. He gripped the handle tighter now, stood up and inched back, preparing to escape before it attacked.

"You've got to do more than just run, Finn. This thing is fast."

"What is it?"

"*Que ta main ne le réveille pas.*"

"What are you talking about? You can't speak French."

Neil laughed. "I forgot."

"So, what should I do now?"

Neil leaned forward as if telling a secret. "You have to catch it first."

"Catch what? I don't even know what it is."

"Sure you do. But you can't just get up and run away. Learn some French. *Apprends le français avant d'être tué par cette chose.*"

"Learn French... before this thing kills me?"

"Use your brains, Finn. Use them because I didn't." Neil moved his head and touched the empty air where the left side of his brain had been before the "accident."

But Neil was right here, talking to him as if it was no big deal. Just hanging out beside him, offering brotherly advice as if half of his skull weren't missing.

Neil scratched at a patch of flesh on the inside edge of his skull.

Finn cringed and took a little time now to inspect the wound. About half the brain was gone. Loose gray matter hung out like worms where the blast had cut through him. "Doesn't that hurt?"

"It did—at first. Not so much now." Neil laughed. "Kind of itchy, though."

Finn leaned toward his brother. "Where are you?"

"With you, idiot. But I think you mean whether I am in heaven or hell. Neither. But that's not important right now. Focus on the French stuff."

Finn stared again at the figure in the corner. His heart quickened. "I can't learn French in a day, you know. I didn't do so hot in high school."

Neil laughed. "What about your girls in Paris? But, seriously, don't waste your time analyzing this. Time to act."

The thing in the corner moved and stepped out from the shadows now, although every detail of its form remained obscure. It held the outline of a person, but its edges had no definition.

Terror rose in Finn's chest. His heart beat faster as he stood beside the open grave and stared down at Neil's gaping, bloody wound. Finn reached down and tugged on Neil's shoulder. "I think we should go."

"It doesn't want me. It's got its eyes on you."

Finn stared at the shadowy form. Yes, he could feel it watching him. It locked its gaze on him, and his skin crawled.

"What are you waiting for?" Neil asked, turning his face up to Finn with wide eyes. He screamed, "Run!"

Finn stumbled away and ran for the door. Shuffling footsteps raced after him, but he didn't look back. The open doorway was just ahead, but it still took far too long to get there.

Rushing outside, he swung around and slammed the metal door shut behind him. As he fumbled with the latch to lock it, the thing slammed against the other side of the door, thrusting it out toward him for a moment before he jammed it shut again. A moment later, he slipped the padlock onto the latch.

The thing was trapped in there now with his brother. Thundering noises erupted from inside the crypt. He considered opening it again to rescue Neil until someone tapped his shoulder.

Finn shuddered, then glanced over. Neil stood beside him in the afternoon light with a solemn smile on his face.

"I trapped it." Finn's heart pounded as he stepped back.

His brother laughed and threw his arm around him. He began squeezing hard. "Not even close."

Finn's eyes burst open, and the gray morning sky slid in through the cracks around the edges of the blinds. Raindrops gently tapped against the window and splashed the windowsill.

His face was wet too. Tears dripped down his cheeks and soaked into the pillow. He cried for a few more minutes, with Neil's face and words still vivid in his mind, until someone knocked on the front door downstairs and pulled him back to reality.

Finn rose like an old man and took his time getting dressed before going downstairs to answer it. Whoever it was could wait. By the time he finally opened the door, he expected the visitor would have given up and moved on, but instead he faced a small, elderly Asian woman dressed in a white raincoat.

8

The old woman smiled broadly, revealing several crooked teeth. "Hi, I'm Betty Wang. I live just up the road." She pointed to a house a few hundred yards away. A small white house obscured by a row of pine trees. "I saw that someone moved in, and I thought it would be nice to meet my new neighbor."

Finn wasn't in the best mood after his dream, but he reminded himself that he might get gossip this time, at least. What else did old ladies in small towns have to do? He shook her hand. "I'm Finn."

The woman nodded slowly, smiling, and shivered a little in her raincoat. Now her vulnerability and age disarmed him. "Do you want to step inside, get out of the rain?"

"Thank you."

She wiped her shoes on the furnished rug in the entryway. "I hope I'm not disturbing you."

Finn disguised a yawn. "No, I was just getting up."

Betty was still shivering.

"Would you like some coffee?" He gestured to the kitchen. "Warm you up a bit?"

She met his gaze and nodded once before removing her raincoat. "Yes, please."

Finn grabbed her raincoat and walked it to the kitchen, draping it over one of the oversized wooden chairs.

Betty took her time getting there, instead looping slowly through the foyer, observing the portraits and doorways along the way. That seemed promising, as she was obviously nosy, which meant she would know things. She paused at the camera and tripod he'd set up earlier. "You brought a lot of electronics with you."

"It's a hobby."

Finn made her coffee as the wind picked up, battering the surrounding windows. Another lightning strike nearby boomed through the house.

The lights flickered, and the walls creaked. Finn glanced at the overhead fixture.

A chuckle by his side startled him. She had approached so quietly. "Wouldn't you be worried, if it wasn't the rain?" she asked.

Her candidness caught him off guard, and he just handed her the mug, curiously waiting for what else she might say.

Betty sat down and sipped her coffee. "This is the best coffee I've had in a while. Maybe it's just because I'm so cold."

"It's special from Colombia." Finn looked around for a thermostat. "True that it's a little chilly in here. I forgot to ask the caretaker how to adjust the heat."

"The old furnace may not be enough to keep you warm."

"You know the house well?"

She shrugged. "I've been in town a while."

Finn sat across from her. "And it looks like you've heard about the ghosts here from what you said before."

Blowing on the coffee, she sipped again. "Who hasn't?"

All right, maybe he was getting somewhere... "Do you think I'll be seeing any?"

"That depends."

"On what?"

"On how badly they want you to see them."

Finn poured himself some coffee. "You know about ghosts?"

She took her time to answer, and when she did, her gaze was level. "I've had a long life."

"Are you a ghost hunter?"

"I think that's you." She chuckled again, motioning back to the living room. "With all that stuff there. Tell me, do you think you can withstand their emotions?"

Leaning back, Finn studied her. This was a different specimen than the caretaker and the neighbors. She cut to the chase, so he did it too. "Why do I get the feeling you aren't here to actually welcome me to the neighborhood, but more to warn me to get the hell out?"

"Maybe you're a little clever. What you find here isn't to be taken lightly. You are familiar with the story of Victor Caine, aren't you?"

Finn nodded. "I made a visit over to the memorial yesterday. I know about the Native Americans slaughtering the settlers, and how he became a big hero. If Victor is haunting this house, what would I have to worry about?"

"The hallways of this house are haunted by the haunted. It's not Victor you need to worry about, so I recommend being very careful with anything you find here. The spirits in this house want revenge, and they don't always care who they take it out on."

"All right. Care to elaborate a little?"

"Nope." Betty pushed the rest of her coffee away while standing up. "You're here alone, right?"

"Yes."

"It'll be interesting to see how long you stay."

"Why is that?" He folded his arms over his chest.

"I'm sure you know. I'm guessing the haunting is the real

reason you rented this place. People who rent Caine House either maintain that ghosts are nonsense or have a fascination for them. And you look like a thrill seeker. Better buckle up."

"Is that a promise?"

Shaking her head a little, Betty stepped over to the kitchen counter where Finn had unpacked a box of his things. Along the back stood a row of porcelain figurines he had brought with him. She turned them over in her hands, studying each one. She paused on his Japanese Shoki figurine first.

"Do you think this will protect you?" Betty asked.

"I just picked it up on a trip."

"It won't do any good here." She took his Hindu figurine next. "And this one? An amulet?"

"Well, I admit I'm a little superstitious."

"The Hindu goddess Durga. In some situations she can protect you from harmful spirits, but there's too much darkness in this house for her to make much difference. I would recommend you to leave, or at least leave most of your items packed up and ready to go. You might end up having to run like the previous tenants, and it would be a shame to have gone through all that work of settling in."

Finn leaned against the counter and grinned. "But if you know I came to see *things* then you know you're only whetting my appetite."

"You are cocky, like a teenager." Betty again shook her head and gave a sigh, as if speaking to a stupid pupil at school. "None of the stuff you've brought will be any help. You know something, not a lot, about ghosts, and you should take these seriously."

"Thank you for your advice." Finn rolled his eyes when she glanced away. His mood had returned to bad, bordering on belligerent, as he never liked to be told what to do; or what not to do. Especially by strangers.

Unfazed by his tone, Betty took her coat and stepped toward the door. "Another piece of advice, and this one is crucial: Sometimes objects have a purpose for their location. Best to leave them undisturbed as much as possible. Everything where it is, especially what is fixed. It's in your best interest." Before she walked out, putting her coat back on, she added, "If you can't be wise, try being smart."

Betty left, and as soon as the door shut something crashed against the floor upstairs. Not a door slamming or footsteps or some tapping on the glass. This was like the noise of a three-hundred-pound man collapsing. Finn grabbed his thermal camera and ran up the stairs—no time to take anything else. He switched it on as he raced toward the source of the noise—his bedroom. Throwing the door open, he expected to find either an intruder or more paranormal activity. Peering at everything through his camera, an icy chill passed over him, as if someone had just left as he entered.

If it had occurred only a few minutes earlier, Betty would have been there to see it. Would she have joined him in exploring the source, or sneered at his excitement?

Thunderous stomping over the hallway floor made it seem like the ghost wore massive boots. It raced down the stairs. More footsteps joined the first. Not just one spirit in the house, for sure.

Finn followed the sounds, keeping an eye on the screen of his thermal camera. Pockets of blue revealed something hovering in the air ahead of him as he stopped at the top of the stairs, looking down. A blue silhouette shifted and faded until disappearing.

Another sound from the upstairs hallway caught his attention. This one echoed like someone cocking a gun behind one of the guest room doors. Finn's heart raced as he forced himself to hurry back into the closed room with the camera up and ready. He threw open the door, convinced someone would be standing in there, ready to confront him. The room was empty, but it did nothing to ease his pounding heart. This was exactly what he'd hoped for. So why had the spirits not acted up like this the night before?

Betty's words came back to him. *They'll find you.*

Looks like they found me, Betty.

He ran to his phone and called Emmie. She and Sarah needed to get over right away and see this.

❧ 9 ❧

As soon as Emmie walked through the doorway of Caine House, the smell struck her. Not a *foul* smell, but instead something that stirred up memories of visiting her grandmother's house long ago, or the early days of moving into the Hanging House. It was all the old wood and the stale air.

Emmie cringed. "You might want to open the windows in here for an afternoon."

"I had the same thought." Sarah sniffed the air and gazed at Finn. "Can't you smell it?"

Finn sniffed too, with a confused expression. "Not really. It's probably just the antiques. But an old place like this won't smell like roses."

Emmie held her throat and acted as if she were gagging. "We'll get you some air fresheners."

"You can decorate the whole place if you want. I just need you to tell me if I'm wasting my time here."

"Hey, we're not one of your devices, you know."

"Sorry, I said that wrong. Please... help me." Finn pressed his hands together as if praying to them.

"That's better." Sarah smirked.

Emmie walked beside Sarah into the foyer and took in everything around her. It was like a step back in time. She'd heard all the stories of Caine House; most people in the area had, but she'd never had a desire to visit it. There had been enough confrontations with spirits in her daily life without seeking them out.

Despite the house's age, it was in fine shape, and it impressed her that it had survived over the years so well. Victor Caine had surrounded himself with the finer things back then, and it showed.

The town of Lake Eden hadn't shied away from advertising the historical significance of their local legend either, even holding an annual festival in his honor called "Caine Daze." As a child, her school had taken a bus field trip to Lake Eden to visit the towering statue of Mr. Caine at City Hall, the Monument to the Innocents, Caine Industries, and stopping last at Caine House. Emmie had dodged that trip by feigning sickness, and her parents had still pressured her, emphasizing the chance to "practice her skills in a wider capacity," but they'd backed down after she'd agreed to try communicating with the Hanging Girl for the rest of the day.

"So what did the landlord say when you told him you were hunting for ghosts?" Sarah asked.

Finn shrugged. "No need to tell him anything or show him any equipment he might object to, although he says he doesn't believe any of the stories."

Emmie grinned and ran her hand across the carved wood corner of a wall. "What stories?"

"You know, the ghosts."

"How do you know they're true? Not all ghost stories are true, you know, or so some guy in a library once told me."

"Ha-ha. Except that this morning I heard all kinds of weird things like in your house. Footsteps and thumps on the floor upstairs. Even spurs."

Emmie turned to Sarah. "What do you think?"

Sarah grinned. "Yes, sounds like a ghost, all right."

Finn groaned. "Okay, are you telling me it would not be fun for us to be the three musketeers again and go through the house together?"

"Three musketeers?" Sarah hooted with laughter.

"And we use our abilities to track down a ghost for you, right?" Emmie asked, also laughing.

"Listen, this morning I ran into more paranormal activity than I have ever experienced in all the years I've been looking... Well, except for your house. The Hanging House set the standard for paranormal activity, in my book. But this place is the real deal... I hope."

Emmie walked over to one of the walls and stared at the large painting of Victor standing in a suit and tie with his hands at his side and a look like he had just conquered Rome. Beside the portrait, a small black and white family portrait showed a man and woman standing behind two young boys. The youngest boy had the same eyes as Victor. *Is that him?*

Sarah came up beside her. "Good-looking guy."

A big *HA!* from Finn made them both turn. He motioned to the paintings. "That's good-looking?"

"Yeah, like Christopher Plummer in *The Sound of Music,*" Sarah said, studying Victor again.

Finn shook his head. "I don't see the resemblance, and that film is almost as old as this town. I'm just sick of seeing him."

"Don't worry, Finn, you're as handsome as—"

"Stop." He held up a finger.

Emmie and Sarah exchanged a playful look.

Finn stepped away from the paintings. "Do you see anything?"

Emmie glanced around. "Not yet."

Sarah half closed her eyes and swayed a little. "I feel turbulence, though. Like... anger? And there's more than one spirit nearby."

Finn's face lit up. "That's what that other woman said."

"What other woman?"

"Betty someone. Betty Wang, I think. An old Asian woman. She stopped by this morning when it was raining. I thought she was just the typical small-town nosy..."

Emmie glared at Finn.

"Sorry. It's just that instead she was sharp as hell, talked about the ghosts in the house and basically warned me to get ready."

"Ready for what?"

"Buckle up for the emotions, she said. And she *did* say that they would find me."

Sarah looked worried for a moment. "How does she know that?"

"She was sharp, like I said, and she knew about amulets from all over the place. She could tell right away I was hunting ghosts."

"Betty Wang," Emmie repeated the name under her breath. "Why does it sound familiar?"

Finn shrugged. "Lots of people named Wang in China, and in the US. And probably a lot of Betty Wangs too."

Emmie furrowed her brow. "I guess. It just sticks out in my mind."

Finn continued, "I figure the ghosts are all those Native Americans that Victor killed coming back to get revenge on him somehow. Do you see any Native Americans in this place?"

Emmie glanced around. "Like I said, not a soul." She turned to Sarah. "Do you have any feelings about that?"

Sarah shrugged. "I feel something, a powerful emotion, but I can't tell where it's coming from." But she had gone pale, and she lowered her head. "I might need to go outside for a while. It's been a little overwhelming lately."

"Sure." Finn stepped toward her. "Get some fresh air. I'll be out there in a minute."

Sarah walked out the front door and stood with her back to the door.

Emmie waited until Sarah was out of hearing range before

saying, "Her grandmother passed away after a stroke, two days ago. They were close."

"Oh, I'm sorry to hear that." He glanced toward Sarah, his face softening. "My uncle had a stroke, and it was devastating for him, and everyone."

"Yes, I think it really affected Sarah. She was at the hospital when it happened. Maybe she..."

They looked at each other. Emmie saw that Finn had understood. *Maybe Sarah had helped her grandmother pass.*

"Damn," he mumbled. "Death and ghosts might be too much for her now."

"She wanted to come. She took a few days off work to relax."

Again Finn looked at Sarah. "Not sure this will be relaxing. We'll keep an eye on her, and you make sure to tell me if you want to leave."

"Right," she said with a deep breath. Sarah was still outside, pacing a little. "Back to business. Tell me more about what happened this morning."

He glanced up at the ceiling. "All right, so all the noises came from upstairs. Would you mind going there with me?"

Emmie feigned a coy look. "Go upstairs with you? I thought you'd never ask."

"Flirt."

"Okay, Casanova, lead the way."

Finn led her upstairs, and she paused along the way to stare at some of the framed photos and paintings. Nothing particularly strange.

"I'm surprised these are still in the house. I mean, it's a rental house, not a museum."

"That was part of the deal. The caretaker made it very clear that everything was to stay, and I was responsible for making sure nothing gets damaged. He took a hefty security deposit and even my credit card number, just in case."

Emmie spotted one of Finn's cameras attached to a tripod in the corner. "I see you're all set up already."

"Partially. It's still going to take some time to get everything operational and organized." He held his arms out like he was presenting something wonderful. "This is a dream come true for me. At least I hope it will end up better than what the old woman suggested earlier. I've got six months to find the spirits in this house."

"She didn't seem to think it would take this long, from what you said."

"I guess we'll see."

At the top of the stairs were a few more framed photos of various landscapes. All of them were black and white, showing fields and properties and families of days gone by. Along the bottom of one photo, it read, "Lake Eden, 1898." Another wall had an old grandfather clock, although the pendulums weren't swinging.

Emmie cringed at the ornate wallpaper. "How would you like to remove all of this?"

"Absolutely not."

"You said I could decorate."

"If you find me ghosts."

"Maybe you could buy this place and renovate it. Think about it. Here's your chance to own a real haunted house, not just rent it."

Finn met her gaze and beamed. "*Or* I could ask you girls to clear out the ghosts, and I'd have a great property at a fantastic price."

Emmie pretended to check the time on her cellphone. "We charge by the hour, you know."

His eyes widened meaningfully. "Let's get moving then."

She followed him as he opened each door along the way. All of them were furnished with a bed and a dresser, the blankets and pillows carefully laid out so that they resembled hotel rooms.

"Victor's room, or mine, is straight ahead." Finn continued to the end of the hall.

Through the open door of the last room, she spotted a sprawling mass of Finn's personal possessions and electronic devices, along with a stack of empty boxes. Beyond that, the woodwork and antiques captivated her.

"Ignore the mess, please." He grinned.

Emmie ran her fingers over the carved molding of the headboard and along the edges of the dresser. All of it hand carved. Even a few of the photos on the wall had sculpted wooden frames. "He was definitely rich."

"Very rich. I went into town yesterday and visited the Monument to the Innocents over by Caine Industries. Obviously, he did very well for himself in his day."

"Well, then, I hate to break it to you, but you might have rented a haunted house with no ghosts."

Finn sneered and smiled at the same time. "You still don't see anyone?"

"No one. No sign of anything unusual."

Walking over to one of the two windows, she looked out to the yard below. Finn came up and stood beside her. The yard sprawled for hundreds of feet, stopping at a stream that divided the lawn from a massive cornfield. A smaller stone structure stood at the edge of the property. Emmie pointed to it. "What's that?"

Finn's face changed into a mixture of interest and worry. "I think it's a grave."

"A grave? In Victor's backyard?"

"I found the key to open the place up, and it has a cement slab and a grave marker." He paused as if to think, then asked, "Do you see anyone hovering around down there?"

Emmie scanned the yard again and even focused on the field beyond it. "Nobody. But let's go down there and check it out."

They went downstairs and found Sarah across the living room, staring at the largest portrait of Victor Caine, as if mesmerized by his stare. She stood frozen in place without blinking.

"You okay?" Finn asked.

"That was the weirdest thing." Sarah didn't look away from Victor's portrait.

"What thing?" Emmie asked.

They hurried over to her. Sarah didn't answer, but she didn't need to. Victor's eyes were black holes, as if someone had taken a knife and gouged them out.

❧ 10 ❧

Emmie glanced around the room. Nobody there, physically or not.

Finn looked pale, although he joked, as usual: "There goes my security deposit."

Emmie turned to Sarah. "Did you see or feel anything?"

Sarah shook her head. "I still have that angry feeling, but I thought I felt a little better after being outside for a while."

"Something strange is going on."

"The eyes were definitely not like that," Finn said after a hard swallow. "Do you believe me now?"

"Let's see if someone is around."

"Like Betty Wang," Finn mumbled as he scanned the ceiling and walls.

Emmie veered off in a different direction, walking around the room and opening each door in the area. Just a couple of closets and a shortcut into the back of the house.

After they searched the various areas of the lower level, they regrouped at the front door.

"You may be in luck after all, Finn." Emmie nodded at him. "Keep your cameras ready."

He only nodded, his eyes still scanning the living room.

"Let's go out back and see what that grave is all about," Emmie proposed.

Finn was silent again, staring back at the defaced portrait of Victor. She opened her mouth to repeat herself, but he finally turned toward her and agreed.

Outside, they comforted Sarah on the steps. She insisted she felt better and joined them as they circled around the house, passing several enormous trees that must have been there for at least one hundred years. The air was humid, and the grass damp from the rain showers earlier. A sloping hill of grass led them across the yard down toward the river.

Several pine trees surrounded the stone structure. The trickle of water moving through the stream came from behind a wall of tall grass. They walked up to the stone crypt, as Finn had called it, and stopped at the metal door.

"So there is a grave in there?" Sarah asked.

"Yeah. It's not marked with a name or anything, but I'm sure that's what it is."

"What's a grave doing out here at Caine House?" Sarah paused. "Shouldn't it be at a cemetery?"

"Maybe the town didn't have an official cemetery back whenever this person died," Emmie said. "I know of a few places around Green Hills where they buried someone near an old house or in the churchyard."

Sarah tilted her head to the side. "I've never heard of anyone being buried at their house."

Finn dug out the key and unlocked the door. "I'm sure the caretaker didn't want me to find this."

"Why not?" Sarah asked.

"Probably has enough problems renting the house without this revelation. If people find out about a grave, nobody will want to rent it."

"How did you get the key?" Sarah asked.

"Rummaging around."

"Of course."

The door squeaked open, and Finn used his cellphone like a flashlight to lead them inside. "It's there." He pointed to the far side of the stone structure.

They walked over to it and inspected it together. Emmie leaned down, using her own cell phone to focus on the ornate iron cross that lay on the floor of the structure, near the head of the grave. She picked it up with some difficulty—its weight surprised her. Someone had built that cold, solid relic to last. And she was far from an expert on grave markers, but the workmanship was uniquely ornate—Victorian? Maybe that sort of design was common back then. No name on the cross. Just some French words across the arms, and the bottom end was melted as if a welder had seared through it.

"It says 'Death has closed these eyes'," Finn told her. He looked away before adding, "'May your hand not awaken them.' Or him or her."

"The French doesn't say whether it's male or female? Who do you think it belongs to?" Sarah asked. "Maybe Victor's wife? Or one of his children?"

"Victor never married, apparently, and I didn't read anything about him having children."

Emmie glanced around the space. "Well, I don't see any ghosts here either, children or adults, so I'm guessing the person died from natural causes." She looked toward Sarah. "What are your feelings now?"

Sarah looked pensive, her face a little pinched. "It feels... empty. Hollow. It's strange, but those are the words that occur to me."

Emmie shrugged, and Finn frowned.

"I'm not sure how we could find out who it belongs to," Emmie said. "If this is the source of the noises you heard this morning, Finn, I don't sense a spirit now. But I still don't see adults all that well yet, really. If there was foul play in this death, I guess if you stick around long enough you'll probably get your answer."

Turning his head, Finn stared at Sarah for a long moment, as if he wanted to say something. But when Emmie caught him watching her, he looked sheepish. Under her steady gaze, he smiled and said, "Empty. That's funny."

"Why?" Emmie asked sharply.

He opened his mouth, then bit his bottom lip. *He's holding something back.*

But it was Sarah who broke the silence. She groaned and said, "Hey Emmie, I might need to step outside again."

Apparently relieved, Finn focused on Sarah. "Nauseous?"

She nodded. Her face was even whiter. Not a good sign.

Finn was nearly always attentive, especially toward Sarah, but now he gave her a hug and kept one arm around her as they stepped outside. "Maybe Emmie should take you back home."

"Yeah."

"We've still got months to explore this place."

"I'll get you home, Sarah. Let me just do one thing first." Emmie turned her attention back to the cross lying on the ground. She stepped over and took a picture of it. "That's very interesting. I'll see if I can find out anything about it."

Hurrying back outside, she came up beside Sarah across from Finn.

"I'll walk you back to the car," he said.

Sarah gave a pained smile. "Sorry, Finn. I'm not fun lately."

"Don't worry, I'm sure if there are ghosts here, they'll still be here when you come back."

"Oh, thanks." Sarah chuckled.

Finn locked the door to the crypt.

"Anything else you want to tell us before we leave?" Emmie asked.

He didn't turn for a second, and when he did, he was putting the key in his pocket and running a hand through his hair while he avoided facing her.

"*Anything,* Finn?"

"No, that's it." Now he looked at her and beamed. "Sorry I

dragged you out here just for this. I recorded some things, but I still need to review them. I just thought there'd be more, you know, activity."

"Don't feel bad for the lack of ghosts, Finn," Emmie said firmly. "If it turns out this is just an old house with squeaky floors and drafty walls, you should be happy about it."

"Maybe," he mumbled, looking around.

She put her arm around Sarah's back as they walked around the side of the house toward the front. They reached the car and got in, and she lowered the window and called out, "Later, Finn. Be wise."

"Wish people would stop saying that." His voice wavered—he seemed more haunted than the house.

F inn sat at the kitchen table with his audio recorder and a few other instruments, listening to the sounds of his recordings from the previous day.

How was he going to tell Emmie and Sarah that he'd unscrewed the cross from its place and it had practically exploded? And that Betty Wang had later told him not to move objects, especially if they were fixed. *And* that things had become decidedly livelier in the house after the cross went flying off.

He took in a deep breath. It could all just be a coincidence, but he needed to go back to the crypt and have a look at that hole for traces of gunpowder or a booby trap before he worried Emmie—and especially Sarah, in her state.

"It's your vanity, fool."

Neil would have said something like that, and Finn could hear him as clearly as if he were standing there.

"Right, as usual," Finn answered to the still air of the kitchen.

Motivations were never simple, and he didn't want to preoccupy his friends when they had their own problems, but it was true: He'd done something at least a little stupid. And if they found out—*when* they found out—he'd be in for a lecture.

For now, though, he was alone in the house again, and the vast emptiness thrilled him. Too many rooms to explore with just the few devices he owned. Now would be a good time to expand his arsenal. Maybe put one in each room? It might get expensive, but he had made a commitment to stay there for six months, so maybe that was necessary to take advantage of the situation while he had the chance.

The muffled noises he'd obtained with the audio recorder disappointed him. It hadn't picked up the sounds he'd expected. He must have turned it in the wrong direction or placed it in a poor location. If he could just figure out whether there was a rhyme or reason to the sounds... Some pattern he might duplicate to rule out the usual disturbances like bad plumbing or rodents in the walls. He had been inside enough haunted houses to know most of them were false alarms, but after his experience in Emmie's house, he knew spirits were real. It was more about locating them and capturing the data on his devices. A variation on fishing. Catch and release.

With his headphones on and his eyes closed, he focused on the sounds he had, which were the best part and the worst. The worst because he had to focus on and analyze every second of the recording, and that took up a lot of time. The best was when his patience paid off and he discovered something. Analyzing it on his laptop made it easier, as he could scan through the recordings quickly to the areas where the software pinpointed the disturbances for him. He could watch for the telltale signs of spiking graphs, and jump to each "bite" without listening to all the empty noise in between.

He scrubbed through the software's timeline, stopping on one of the louder noises—several footsteps like a heavy man in boots stomping up the stairs. If only he had set up his video camera to film that area, maybe he could have matched up sounds with some video anomaly. Next time. He listened again. The footsteps rose in intensity, five steps in all, rhythmically rising and falling until fading away. Again. Were those spurs? He listened for voices this time, turning up the audio and adjusting the filters to focus on the subtle frequencies. Was that a man's voice or the wind whistling through the cracks in the window? He listened carefully to a low moan like an old man grumbling—

A sudden knock on the door made him jump in his chair.

He sighed and leaned away from his laptop before slipping off his headphones and standing up. Another neighbor stopping by to meet the crazy idiot who had rented a haunted house.

Building up some patience and forcing a smile, he opened the front door to find a young woman on the steps. The clouds had parted overhead, and the sun brightened the surrounding landscape. She smiled warmly and peered at him with bright blue eyes. Her auburn hair flowed over the shoulders of her bohemian white-lace dress, which descended almost to her brown boots. Three rings of exotic silver necklaces accented with turquoise stones hung around her neck.

"Hi." Finn tried not to stare, as she was more beautiful than the usual girl next door.

"Hello, sorry to bother you. I'm Josie, and I usually wouldn't just knock on someone's door like this, but..." She extended her hand, and he shook it, maybe holding it a little too long. "I saw there was a new person moving in and I'd like to welcome you to the area."

"Nice to meet you."

"You're not afraid to live in this place?"

Another one who cut to the chase. Finn feigned ignorance, as he would not mind trying to get some gossip out of *her*. "Should I be?"

Her eyes widened. "You haven't heard all the stories?"

"Stories?"

"Oh, come on." She chuckled. "You must know. I'm scared just to stand here right now."

She had an accent, too. Something European.

"It's a little spooky," he said in full friendly mode. Finn

looked at her fingers. Only one silver ring on her right hand. *Nice.* "It's just a house."

"So you haven't seen any ghosts?"

"Ghosts?" He gave a laugh that sounded fake even to him, then cleared his throat. "Not yet."

Josie inched back. "Well, I didn't want to disturb you."

"Not at all. Do you like coffee?"

Her smile broadened. "Yes, especially if it's sweet."

Finn laughed. "I think I can rustle up some sugar for you. Come on in, and maybe have a look around, if you dare?"

She stiffened, then nodded. "Yes, I'm going to take that dare."

That sounded funny and formal in her accent. She followed him inside, then around to the kitchen, and once more Finn started making coffee for a neighbor, a little more willingly this time. "I don't drink a lot of coffee, but I keep it around for friends and the occasional craving, or for when I need to work late into the night. Thank God for caffeine."

Josie studied the devices on the table. "What is all this?"

"I'm just working on some stuff. Push it aside if you want."

She didn't touch anything, but sat down and kept her hands in her lap as she glanced around the room. "So this is it?"

"This is it. Ignore the mess, I just moved in."

"I know. I saw you earlier, but I didn't want to bother you."

"You're not a bother. But you're not the first one to stop by either. I guess this house is more popular than I thought."

"It's been here forever. The oldest house in town."

"Do you know much about it?" Taking the coffee and the sugar over to her, Finn gestured to a portrait of Victor nearby. "About him?"

She stared at Victor. "A little."

"Okay, so why would he haunt this place?"

She began putting sugar in the coffee, and she wasn't joking when she said she liked it. He counted six spoonfuls before she started stirring it.

"I'm not so sure it's him," she said with a pout. Oh, she was definitely French. No one pouted like French women. "Do you know about the other men who avenged the settlers?"

He snapped back to what she was saying instead of looking at the lips saying it. "What? Yes. I mean, I read about them and saw them in photos." He nodded at one of the walls. "They're in a painting there, too."

Her blue eyes seemed to glint. "They all died—hanged or shot themselves around Victor's yard."

"Oh, God." Finn glimpsed a tree in the yard outside the kitchen window. "All at the same time?"

She shook her head and crossed her legs. "Slowly. One by one, it is said, they came over and did the suicide. One after another."

Finned leaned back. Men and boots. Several men. And spurs? Could Victor's cronies be the ghosts?

"Why?" he asked out loud.

"Pardon?" she responded in French.

The language shift caught him off guard, but didn't surprise him. "So you *are* French. I thought so."

"Oui. Sorry, yes. Sometimes I jump back and forth without realizing it. What were you saying?"

"I was just wondering why they would all kill themselves. Do you think the Native Americans they killed haunted them?"

A pretty shrug. "Maybe... who knows?"

Finn took a sip of his coffee. "So you believe in ghosts?"

"Absolutely. I mean, I haven't seen any without the aid of my devices, but I know they exist. I wouldn't want to see one, though. That would really scare me." Josie laughed nervously.

"I can relate. Probably better not to seek them out."

"I'm even afraid to look over..." She pointed to the back wall near one of Victor's larger portraits, but kept her eyes on Finn, "because something might be standing there."

Hair rising on the back of his neck, Finn looked behind him, then turned and smiled at her. "I don't think you need to worry."

He indicated his devices. "I've been hunting ghosts for years and the first one I saw—well, I saw it through one of these—was a month ago. They hide, so not much chance we'll see one today."

Josie ran her delicate fingers over the edge of his laptop. "That's good. Let me tell you, I'm so afraid of ghosts that when passing by the cemetery, especially the one up the road where they buried Victor Caine, I always cross the street to avoid it. Maybe one of them will follow me home, I think. Is that crazy?"

"No, not crazy. Maybe a little superstitious."

She indicated one of the devices with her chin. "What does this thing do?"

"That's my audio recorder. Nothing special, but I record the sounds around graves over long periods of time and come back later to see if I've captured any interesting noises."

"Like screaming or moaning?" She imitated the classical sound of a ghost and then laughed.

"Something like that. For instance, I found the grave out behind the house here and I'm planning to leave that device next to it overnight, and when I come back the next morning I'll analyze the data on the laptop."

"A grave back there?" Her eyes widened.

"Inside that smaller building out back."

She cringed. "Who could they have buried here?"

"I guess sometimes people used to bury their loved ones on their own property, but there is no name on it."

"A ghost with no name..." she repeated softly, her eyes shining.

"I don't think you need to worry. Most paranormal activity happens at night for some reason—maybe it's the darkness that allows them to be seen. Our senses are heightened at night, more attuned to primal threats."

"Oh," she exclaimed suddenly, seeing the book. *"Mais c'est en français?"* Her hand hovered over it. *"Tu lis ça? Tu parles français?"*

He got the gist of what she was asking him, whether he was

reading that. "*Un petit peu,*" he said, and made a face. "Lousy accent."

"*Non, non.*" She laughed, the sound like merry little bells. "*Tu es mignon.*"

I'm... cute? His lip curled, but as she kept looking over the book, he decided to frighten her a little more. That way, she wouldn't think he was cute. "It's all about death and revenge and dominion over the underworld..."

"*Oui...*" she murmured, flipping through the pages.

"I had to swear I wouldn't read it aloud when I borrowed it."

She was silent for a moment, then asked. "Whose book is it?"

"A friend's."

Raising her eyes slowly, she asked, "A girl friend?"

"No. I mean, she's a girl—a woman. And she's my friend. But not *petite amie.*"

A smile widened on her face, and it was promising, so Finn went on. "Maybe, as a matter of fact, you could help me translate some of the stuff in the book."

The pout again, and she put it down and pushed it away. "You said it's dangerous."

"Didn't say dangerous."

"All this, you know, death and grave and cemetery..." She shuddered. "*Je n'aime pas.*"

"I get that you wouldn't like it, but it's where we are all headed."

She covered her face but gave a laugh, bigger than he'd expected from her. "But how can you say this?"

"It's true. It's like being afraid of skulls, when there are two in the room right now. Yours and mine."

"*Arrête!*" she squealed. "*Tu es méchant!*"

Méchant, evil or mean, was better than cute.

"You should get over your fears," he continued like he was some sort of expert. "You've gone into a cemetery before, right?"

"Only for a couple of funerals. I don't go there at night." She threw him a sideways glance. "You've gone there at night?"

"Sometimes. Most cemeteries lock the gates to keep the teenagers out, and to keep people like me from hunting for ghosts." Finn glanced at one of the portraits of Victor, a smaller one showing the man holding a rifle without a grin. Her eyes followed his, narrowing. Did she think the man was handsome too? "You know, the best way to get over your fear is to face it head on. I was planning to visit Victor's grave and record the area. If you want, I could take you along to prove that there's nothing to be afraid of."

She shook her head slowly. "I'm not sure that's something I want to do."

"You came up to the front door of this house, right? And you even came inside without a problem. Something about all this interests you. I could take you there. I've never seen anything scary happen inside a cemetery, aside from maybe a blackbird startling me or a bug crawling on my arm. You could show me the location of Victor's grave."

"You don't need me to find it. It's right there in the center."

"But I'd have to go after the sun goes down to get the best readings on my devices. It'll be dark. Maybe you could guide me to it."

Josie stared at the devices on the table, then met Finn's gaze with a scared look on her face. "You just said that's when ghosts come out!"

"They can't harm us, and I've had tons of experience with them." Just a small exaggeration. He leaned forward a little. "Come on, you want to."

Josie hesitated, but a smile did play at the corner of her lovely lips. "You wouldn't just run off and leave me there, right?"

"Never. I'm a gentleman."

"Oh, le gentilhomme!" She let out another merry laugh. "Why don't I trust you?"

"You should," he assured her. "We'll have a picnic. I'll pick up a bottle of wine."

"You won't find good wine here..."

"Challenge accepted. I'll take wine and a blanket."

She was swinging her foot—a good sign that she was more than halfway convinced. "All right. Now you accept mine."

"What's your challenge?"

"Take the book." She narrowed her eyes with a grin. "You're scared of it, so we'll both be scared."

He tilted his head, considering her. "It's not really necessary, is it?"

"Of course, it is," she said, "because if you scare me, I'll start reading that."

He scoffed. "Done."

She shrugged again. "Then I guess I should be brave and face my fears like you said."

"Tonight?"

Josie nodded.

And it was only after she left that he realized she hadn't touched her coffee at all.

That was it. He was done offering the Colombian. He made a mental note to pick up a more common brand, along with the best wine Lake Eden had to offer.

✢ 12 ✣

Sarah hadn't said a word during their trip back to the house. Instead, she had curled into a ball in the passenger seat, and Emmie had switched off the radio. Although she was sensitive, Emmie could not help but worry about how quickly her health had declined. There was more to it than just grief, but she would not ask Sarah if she had helped her grandmother on.

Should Sarah want to tell Emmie, she would be all ears and all understanding. Sarah was a person who would only do such a thing out of kindness and love, and when she stopped missing her grandmother, she would be at peace.

The silence had allowed Emmie's mind to wander back to Caine House. The name Betty Wang had stuck with her for some reason. She'd heard it before, but she couldn't remember where.

Arriving at the house, Emmie opened the car door for Sarah. "How are you feeling?"

Sarah rubbed her forehead. "I've got a headache."

"You should have a painkiller. Let's get in the house."

Walking back inside, Emmie expected Alice Hyde to greet them from somewhere in the living room, watching them enter *her* house, as she often reminded them. This time, Alice was nowhere in sight. Probably the girl had gone out into the back-yard to do what only ghosts do near the site of their death—hang on. Alice Hyde's behavior was predictable now, and they had gotten to know her well in recent weeks. Not seeing her after entering the house caught Emmie off guard.

Sarah groaned, and Emmie quickly pushed the thought of Alice away as Sarah sat on the living room couch. Emmie grabbed some ibuprofen from a kitchen cabinet near the sink, returning with two pills and a glass of water, and sat on the couch next to her friend. "Maybe you should lie down for a while."

Sarah nodded. "I'll be okay." Her hands trembled as she took the medicine and sank back. "You don't need to worry about me. I'm a nurse, remember? I just need a little time."

Emmie nodded and stood up, not wanting to make her feel uncomfortable. "Okay then, I'll just be right here."

Emmie stepped over and sat down at her desk. Now that all her property had arrived, she had a desk again, and she had placed it in the far back corner of the living room, where her mother's desk had been years ago. She turned on her laptop and, while waiting for it to start up, thought of the name again. It stuck at the edge of her mind and teased a connection that she knew existed in her memory somewhere. A former teacher? A neighbor? A celebrity?

Opening her computer browser window, she did an Internet search for Betty Wang and found too many, as Finn had suspected. She wrote Betty Wang + Lake Eden and... Got it. A newspaper article revealing that she had become head librarian at Lake Eden Public Library in the same year her parents had died. One obscure picture of the woman, distant and slightly out of focus, showed a small and somewhat rotund Asian woman with glasses and a pageboy haircut, surrounded by stacks of books.

Looking up the library's website, Emmie went through the

staff, finding a different photograph with the notice that Betty Wang had retired the year before.

And, now in focus, the face was hauntingly familiar. Betty Wang. Haunting... She had something to do with her parents. Then it hit her: The woman's clothes had thrown her off—far too normal. Betty hadn't dressed like that long ago. Back then, far back in Emmie's childhood, Betty had worn colorful dresses and sparkling jewelry that jingled with each step.

"It's her."

Sarah raised her head after a moment. "Who?"

"The woman Finn talked to. Betty Wang. My parents knew her. She was like them, except she was *really* out there. She came over to meet me, and I remember how she asked me a lot of questions."

"What sort of questions?"

"About my gift, although she tried to make it all casual. As if she was getting there, but slowly so as not to scare me. I remember thinking she was strange. Her eyes were intense. And my parents acting as if her opinion was super important."

"Is she dangerous?"

Emmie shrugged. "Who knows? But she was involved in the occult. Some kind of mentor to my parents."

Sarah got up from the couch and came over to Emmie's laptop, standing beside her. "She looks so harmless."

"Maybe she is now, I don't know, but I never felt safe around her. I remember feeling like she could take me away, and my parents would let her."

"Don't children feel stuff like that, sometimes? That they could be abandoned?"

Emmie bit her lip and considered it. "I can't pinpoint what made me feel that. If it was something I overheard or just an impression."

"Is this something we should call Finn about?"

She looked back into the old eyes of Betty Wang. Sharp eyes, all right, but she was still half Finn's height. "I don't think she is an actual danger to him. We can mention it tomorrow."

The door to Sarah's apartment at the back of the house opened, and they glanced toward the sound. Alice Hyde poked her head out from behind the door and stared at Sarah.

"It's okay." Emmie motioned for her to come in. "We're only talking."

Alice stood motionless, but didn't look away from Sarah. "Something's wrong with her."

Emmie nodded. "Sarah's not feeling well. Her grandmother died recently. You can come in if you'd like."

But Alice remained behind the door and stared at Sarah for a few more seconds before shaking her head and returning to the apartment. The door clicked shut behind her.

"Maybe she senses your loss," Emmie said, shrugging.

Sarah managed a big sigh. "Yes... That would resonate with her spirit and feel uncomfortable. I'm sure she doesn't like to be reminded of death."

❧ 13 ❧

At nine forty-five p.m., there was a knock on the door. Just as expected, Josie stood there, wearing the white dress and a broad smile. "Ready to go?"

He opened the door for her and waved her in. "I need to grab stuff."

She stepped in and followed him in around to the kitchen. "Shouldn't we wait until midnight or something like that?"

"There's nothing that says ghosts only come out at midnight. Just a child's fairytale. You nervous?"

"I told you, I don't even like to be there in the daytime."

"Nothing to be afraid of."

"Don't forget the book." She nodded toward it.

"Oh, the guarantee," he said, smirking. He lifted a bottle of wine, not letting her read the label so she couldn't critique it, and two glasses, which he put into a basket meant for laundry. A blanket was already inside.

He held the door open for Josie; her white dress fluttered in the evening air as they stepped outside. The night was warm and buzzing with insects in the surrounding fields. The full moon lit the area, but clouds crept through the sky, threatening to obscure the ambient light.

She paused on the sidewalk and waited for him to catch up, extending her hand. "I am going to hold on to you tonight."

He took hers. *Don't mind if you do.*

They walked through the darkness, and he watched her from the corner of his eyes. She was so graceful in her walk, as if she might break into a ballet at any moment. Her jewelry jingled softly, and an intoxicating scent of lavender filled the air. Under the moonlight, her face looked white and perfect. Her hand felt soft and a little cold in his.

He cleared his throat. "I hope you didn't have to walk too far to get here in this darkness. I could have picked you up."

"The darkness isn't what scares me, just what might be in it."

Finn swatted at some mosquitos buzzing around his face. "The bugs didn't bother you?"

"Not really."

"You're lucky. They seem to like me tonight."

"It's because you're so sweet." She squeezed his hand.

Before they arrived at the car, Finn hurried forward and opened the passenger side door.

She touched his face as she climbed inside. *"Mon gentilhomme."*

Finn circled around to the driver's seat. As he started the car, the stereo kicked in and blared loud rock music he'd been listening to during his last drive.

He switched it off and grinned. "Sorry about that."

"It's all right. I like all kinds of music, but I prefer the older ballads."

"Like classic rock? Led Zeppelin?"

She shrugged. "Do you recognize this?" She started singing in a high, clear voice:

"L'amour est un oiseau rebelle
Que nul ne peut apprivoiser
Et c'est bien en vain qu'on l'appelle
S'il lui convient de refuser..."

"Opera?" he said, nodding in appreciation. *"Carmen,* I think?"

She was smiling. "It's a favorite of mine. I saw it once, in Paris."

"What does it say?"

"You speak a little French."

"I understood *amour* and *oiseau*. Love and a bird."

"Love is like a rebellious bird, and it doesn't come when you call..."

Finn chuckled. "Story of my life."

Finn pulled out of the driveway onto the winding main gravel road leading back in toward town. Josie didn't wear her seatbelt, but there wasn't much traffic at that time, and he wasn't going to make an issue of it.

European girls... Culture and a healthy disregard for the rules. A perfect mix of attractive qualities.

She glanced over at him. "You didn't bring any of your devices. What will you do if we see a ghost tonight?"

"Probably run away, right after you. But it's better for me to stay focused on more important things, like getting to know you better."

"Lovely. What would you like to know?"

His thoughts drifted back to first meeting her. "Do you live far from Caine House?"

"Not far." Her voice was tense, and a moment of silence hung in the air.

More nervous than I thought. What could he say to ease her mind? He regretted now not offering her some of the wine before they'd left home. "I managed to find a good French wine not too far away. Do you like Pinot noir from Burgundy?"

Her face brightened. "Delightful!"

"I won the challenge then."

She gave him a mischievous grin. "Yes, you did. I think you'll like your reward."

Finn's face warmed as the car rumbled closer to town.

Within a few minutes, he slowed near the cemetery, passing

it on his way to the main city street where he could park in a residential area to avoid unwanted attention.

"We're getting close," he told her.

She immediately sat up and gasped when the tops of the monuments came into view over the fence. "Oh, I've got the goosebumps already."

With her gaze still locked on their destination, she reached out and laid a hand on his thigh.

He lost his breath for a moment. *This is already going well.*

"There it is," Finn said as they passed it.

Finn parked the car away from the streetlights and grabbed a flashlight from his glove compartment.

She handed him the book with a raised eyebrow. "I'll let you carry this."

"Don't you want to keep it handy in case I scare you? That was the agreement, right?"

She stroked his arm. "I trust you."

Better every minute.

He stuffed the book into his waistband again and went for the wine and blanket, but she stopped him.

"We can celebrate our bravery afterwards, no?" she said.

Perfect. He wasn't really going to subject her to a picnic among the graves, anyway. They'd go in, take a look at Victor's grave and run out giggling and in the mood for something else.

In silence, they walked down the block and a half over to the cemetery fence, their path lit only by the moonlight. Finn switched on the flashlight after making sure no cars were approaching and scanned the perimeter for an easier way in. Alone, he could scale the fence without too much trouble, but he doubted Josie would appreciate the climb in her dress.

Josie grabbed the top edge of the metal fence and rattled it. "How will we get in?"

Finn moved ahead of her, eyeing the bars for an opening. "Sometimes kids pull the bars apart so they can sneak in and out.

At least this isn't one of those cemeteries with a brick wall around it. Maybe we'll get lucky. Otherwise..."

The fence clanged and rattled behind him. He spun the flashlight around to check on Josie, but she was gone.

Hell!

A moment later, he caught sight of her white dress through the bars of the fence. She was standing on the other side, inside the cemetery.

His mouth dropped open. "Oh..."

"Just climb over." Her eyes were wide with something other than fear, and she gestured to him. "Hurry!"

❧ 14 ❧

It was as if the box were calling to her. Perhaps it was because she had remembered Betty Wang and her parents, but Emmie walked to the kitchen and then straight to the cardboard box with the word "Recovered" written across the side. The irony in the word struck her again.

After a pause, she flipped open the top.

"You sure you want to look at it now?"

Emmie jumped, not having heard Sarah come up behind her. "Feeling better?"

"Yes. Pain is gone." Sarah leaned her elbows on the counter.

"I am going to have a look."

"All right. What else is inside?"

"I'm guessing precious things." Emmie smirked.

Sarah scoffed. "You might be right."

Emmie pulled out a gray hoodie first. "See what I mean?" She winced as its stale smell filled the air. "That'll need to be washed."

More *precious* items included a set of jumper cables, a toolbox, a plastic bag containing an assortment of her dad's car repair manuals, and a few torn books on the occult. Nothing that would have justified her struggle to carry it into the house.

But something else sat at the bottom. She dug deeper and pulled out an object, large and heavy and wrapped in a muddy red and white quilt. She thought it might be an old-fashioned tire wrench, the kind shaped like a cross, except that it was too thick, and it weighed a ton. Sarah had to help her lift it out. Unwrapping it, Emmie discovered an ornate black cross made of iron, very similar to the one in Finn's crypt.

"Another iron cross?" Sarah asked.

"That *is* strange." Emmie studied it. Woven within each arm of the cross were various occult symbols with the pentagram capping the top. The bottom looked as if designed to be screwed into a base.

"Is it a coincidence?" Sarah murmured.

Emmie didn't answer. The more she studied it, the more it confused her. Some French words were engraved along the arms of the cross. The same words as the cross in the crypt? Setting it on the counter, she pulled out her cellphone and flipped through her pictures of the grave behind Caine House. She zoomed in on the cross. The same words.

"So that's what was so heavy in there," Sarah said.

"I was hoping we'd find gold coins." Emmie brushed away the dirt and turned it over. "But where did it come from?"

"The other was marking a grave."

"That's what we assumed. We don't know for sure." Emmie frowned. "I mean, it would be too much if my parents snatched it out of the cemetery."

"I'm sure they wouldn't take something like that, knowing what they knew about the paranormal."

Emmie shrugged. "They did a lot of strange things."

"Maybe they purchased it or found it somewhere. Should we try to find out where it belongs? What if there's a grave out there missing its cross?"

"Finn said it read something like, 'Death has closed these eyes...'"

"'May your hand not awaken him or her'," Sarah said slowly. "He said it could be either."

Emmie rushed to her desk, and even before sitting she started an Internet search for the French words, looking back and forth between her phone and the browser to spell them correctly. Maybe the words on the cross would reveal some clues as to its origin. The hits she found seemed not close enough, and were leading her away from crosses and graves. Emmie sat down before the laptop while Sarah perched nearby on the arm of the sofa.

"I'm just trying to wrap my head around why two crosses in the same style, with the same words, show up at the same time," Emmie said.

"The words," Sarah said. "They're like a warning. Like saying, don't move me."

"And both were moved, or at least were not on their graves."

She typed faster. Iron crosses, graves, spirits. And there it was...

"In New Orleans, they sometimes used iron crosses to lock a spirit in their grave." A sense of dread washed through her chest. "And my parents crashed near Lake Eden, with a cross like that in their car..."

"They can't have—"

"Released a spirit before their crash? And if they did, could the spirit have attacked them?"

Sarah looked pale in the light of the computer as she considered that possibility.

Emmie glanced over her shoulder and lowered her voice before continuing. Better that Alice didn't hear it. "We know how the spirits can get... violent."

Sarah nodded solemnly. "And the French book was in the box too. That means your parents had it with them."

"They must have been performing some ceremony, and they released the spirit..."

But now Finn had the French book. And an identical cross behind his house.

The answer to Finn's mysterious hesitation at the crypt, his sheepish look, hit Emmie hard. He had done something to that cross. He had messed with it.

She tensed. "We need to go to Finn's house. Right now."

Sarah looked at her with tired eyes. "What's wrong?"

"I think he did something really bad, and he is in a lot of danger."

"How do you know?"

"I'll explain in the car. Start trying to call him. We have to get him out of the house until we get there."

Sarah seemed to gain fresh energy as she pulled out her cellphone and hit the speed dial for Finn. "He's not answering."

Emmie grabbed her keys from the kitchen countertop. "Just keep trying."

Within minutes, they were on the road again, racing to Caine House.

Whatever had killed her parents was still around. Emmie knew this beyond certainty.

🎐 15 🎐

Passing clouds scattered the moon's light overhead as they made their way around the gravestones and trees.

Josie clung to Finn's side. "Victor's grave is near the front. I'm surprised you haven't been here before, since you're a ghost hunter. There are lots of stories about him."

"I haven't been in the town long enough to explore its history very much."

"I'm sure the residents of Lake Eden would flog us if they caught us here after dark. They might think we intended to desecrate their revered founder's grave."

"We'll just need to be careful."

They weaved around a line of white smaller memorials—a family buried together?—but they didn't pause to check the dates on the stones. The grass rustled under their feet until they arrived at a narrow, paved road and made their way toward the front of the cemetery.

"His grave is over there." Josie's voice was somber as she pointed into the darkness ahead.

He slipped his arm around her. "We'll be okay."

The streetlights outside only lit the gravestones near the front of the cemetery, but with all the trees between them, there was little chance anyone would see Finn's flashlight. Still, he didn't intend to take any chances. He aimed the light low and glanced toward the front gate every so often. A few cars passed along Main Street, but the headlights never crossed over into the cemetery. If one were to slow down, it would mean a police car intending to check things out, and they would need to run—something he'd done on a few past occasions.

Finn read some of the names on the memorials as he passed. Robinson, Anderson, Miller, Smith. Common Minnesota names, but the faces of the stones in that section of the cemetery were worn away with time. The dates and epitaphs were barely legible, and some of them had sunk into the ground, angling to one side as if the earth would soon swallow them up.

A little further along, larger and more modern granite memorials provided a better cover for their nighttime intrusion. At least they hadn't seen any *fresh* gravesites. That might send Josie running into the night and screaming.

Finn laughed to himself when Josie stepped ahead of him for a moment and pulled him forward. *She just wants to get this over with.* A kind of brave cowardice.

She directed him around a gravesite with a small stone bench placed near it. Aiming the light off to the side, Finn stumbled over a bouquet of red roses at the base of a gravestone set flat on the ground. It broke Josie's hold on him for a moment before she snatched him back again. He tried to place the flowers back. "Hang on."

"No time." She yanked him forward.

She's frantic to get out of here. Perfect. More time for wine and romance later.

"Prends garde à toi..." she mumbled under her breath in a singsong.

Watch out for yourself. Was she singing that to him?

They crept along through the shadows. Not much chance anyone walking along the street would see them, but the average person, unlike a cop, would run at the sight of figures darting around at night between the gravestones.

Josie pushed close to him at every turn, and he pretended to shelter her from the traffic lights since nothing scary was happening, except for the little opera tune that would break out from her lips every now and again. Sometimes with a laugh.

"How are you feeling?" Finn asked.

"It's not much farther." She pulled on his arm.

She's excited. Okay, one of those kinky types.

A short distance further, Finn spotted it. Victor Caine's grave was just ahead of them in the center of a roundabout. The layered base stood a few feet high and several feet wide. No statue here, but two elaborate pillars reminiscent of the style of his home rose another few feet into the air, and between them stood a wall of carved text into the stone beside a relief of Victor's head. There was no mistaking it. This man was important, and, given all the impressive stories about him, they had spared no expense to glorify his achievements. They had gone all out, even carving elaborate designs into the pillars.

Perched at the top stood a black cross.

On closer look, it was another iron cross, just like the one at Caine House.

He stopped to consider that, but Josie snuggled up again. "I never thought I would see this day."

Pulling back to look at her face, he chuckled. *She's fascinated by this grave.* "You won't pass out on me, will you?"

She grew serious. "I'm not a child, Finn."

"Just kidding around, you know."

She didn't laugh. Her voice lowered by an octave instead. "Do you think Victor Caine is listening to us right now?"

Finn scanned his flashlight over the text on the stone. The inscription telling of Victor's life was like the one at the memorial in front of City Hall. "I doubt it. He died a natural death, according to what I've read, so I'm sure he's moved on by now."

"You think ghosts only stay if they die a violent death?"

"That's the theory."

"The dead can be cursed, for your information. And then they are forced to stay, no matter how they died."

Finn shrugged. "I suppose it could be true. And I guess powerful men always have someone cursing them."

"*Il n'était pas si puissant...*"

He wasn't that powerful...?

A bird cawed overhead, and Finn had to disguise a slight jolt. Josie grabbed hold of his jacket. In the moonlight, their eyes met for a moment. "I'm scared, but I do feel safe with you."

Finn angled the flashlight down as she leaned in, nuzzling her chin up against his. He bent his head and they kissed. He held her tighter, and her hands trembled as she reached under his coat. The book stashed under his belt moved. She smiled against his mouth and backed away. "I'm glad you brought me out here."

Finn moved forward again, but she held him back, a hand over his chest, as she stared up at Victor's memorial. "That's an interesting cross."

Finn followed her gaze. "I agree."

"Beautiful work."

"It must have been a popular style at that time," he said. "I've seen another one."

"Yes..." Josie stepped toward it. "It says something in French."

"Just an epitaph they put on old grave markers, like rest in peace."

"No... More than that. The design is so beautiful. It looks like some massive piece of jewelry up there."

Finn chuckled. "I wouldn't want to hang that around my neck."

She didn't laugh, but instead turned with a wild look on her face, her blue eyes almost neon in the glare of the flashlight, and took hold of his jacket again. "Do you know what would be incredible? To have a souvenir from tonight!"

"Hmm, what kind of souvenir?" She pulled him off balance as she leaned in.

Her lips approached his again, and she bit him softly. "The cross, of course."

"Ha, is that a joke?"

She clenched his jacket a little tighter. "Why would it be a joke? You brought me out here, no? Now I want something to remember the night. I went to a graveyard with a *très bel homme.*" When he didn't move or say anything, she glared into his eyes. "What's wrong?"

He shrugged, staring down at her. "Just that you don't look so scared anymore. You aren't one of them, are you?"

"One of what?"

"One of those New Age would-be psychics who love getting magic stuff out of weird places."

"You said this place was not weird," she sneered. "And maybe I'm less scared and you are more?"

"See," he said, stepping back. "The vibe isn't the same now." He glanced at the cross, then at her. The same hunger was there on her face.

Her voice softened to a low growl. "Please get me the souvenir, Finn."

"Why not go up there and grab it yourself?"

"I will." She pushed Finn out of the way and stepped beside the grave, but stopped.

He nodded. "I'm thinking you brought me out here to get that cross for you because you can't get it yourself..."

"*Sois pas idiot!*" She drew herself up and clenched her fists. The warmth drained from her eyes—no longer the sweet young woman. Now she was a queen demanding his obedience. "Am I wasting my time with you?"

"Strange how I'm thinking the same thing. No other guy in town would come here to steal Victor Caine's cross, had to be the *idiot* who just arrived, right?"

She sneered again. "*Mon pauvre sot...*"

"Why does it matter so much to you? The last time I messed with a cross like that, some freaky things happened."

Moving toward him with a steady gaze and lips pressed together, she let out an exasperated snarl, like a hungry cat, and tossed the flashlight. The light disappeared among the stones as she stormed off into the darkness.

"Josie?"

No answer. For a moment, he considered going after her.

"Hell with it." A bird fluttered in a tree nearby, but this time it didn't scare him.

He found the flashlight and whistled on his way back to the car.

✥ 16 ✥

Finn walked back to his car with a bitter grin on his face.
Another memorable experience in a cemetery, and he
doubted he would forget his failed date anytime soon. This was
one to share with friends over a few beers—several beers.

"You should have known, Finn." He laughed out loud and
rolled his eyes, then mimicked her French accent. "Oh, I'm so
scared, Finn. Please keep me safe."

Another thing he'd rather not tell Emmie and Sarah. He
hadn't even told them about his idiocy with the first cross, and
Josie had almost fooled him into taking a second one. But his
rationality had eventually kicked in, coming to the rescue at the
last minute to steer him back toward reality. *Thank you, brain.
You're welcome, Finn, now let's just slow down a bit, shall we?* Hot
woman or not, he wasn't going to just roll over.

It was better that she'd run off after their altercation, since
the car ride home would have been excruciatingly awkward. The
whole thing had just been an act for whatever bizarre reason. It
wasn't like him to become attached to someone in such a short
time, but her beauty had clouded his common sense, and it
stung.

He could understand someone's fascination with the paranormal world. He was a ghost hunter, after all, but he'd never gone so far as to try seducing someone into getting his way. Occasionally, he'd trespassed on private property to get inside an abandoned building, and had told plenty of lies to get out of trouble. He was no saint. But... what the hell? If her only objective had been to communicate with Victor, or sell the cross, had she really thought a quick seduction and some theater would get her there?

Watch out for yourself. Well, you do that, honey. Good riddance.

He would chalk it up on his scoreboard as just another life lesson learned. Although he made a note to look at the base of that damn cross at Caine House for traces of a booby trap, and to tell Emmie and Sarah about it. If some red-haired French Wicca nut was scavenging the area for an identical cross belonging to Victor Caine, they should know too.

Driving back alone along the same road, he kept an eye out for Josie. She had chosen to walk home alone in the dark with mosquitos probably swarming her and no flashlight, although he did not, he did *not*, want her to apologize or turn sweet again or anything like that.

No sign of her the entire way.

How far could she have gotten on her own? Most likely, she had taken a different route back to her house. Or maybe she had never lived in the area, anyway. She could have parked her car somewhere along a side road near Caine House, and now she had simply driven off, angry at not getting what she wanted.

At the house, Finn carried the flashlight and French occult book inside, as well as the blanket and wine, but before he closed the front door, a series of noises caught his attention. A flurry of sounds, as if a group of people were walking up and down the stairs and someone else was running through the bedrooms upstairs. The door handle slipped from his fingers and crashed shut behind him.

He froze for a moment before running into the kitchen and

grabbing his Beast device off the kitchen table. Scrambling back into the foyer, he switched it on and angled it up toward the noises without looking at the display. His hands shook, and he tried to steady himself as he stepped toward the stairs. The disturbance spread out from the staircase and grew louder within the upper rooms.

He had calmed down in the car, but now his eyes were wide open and his heart pounded. The house was alive, and the activity surrounded him. A bottle on a nearby shelf rattled as if in an earthquake as he stepped into the living room area. Victor's portrait on the wall, with his eyes still gouged out, transformed for a moment, like a lenticular mirage, into Finn's image; now his own eyes were gouged out.

He blinked and... Victor's face reappeared. A trick of the light?

This was the real deal. Paranormal activity everywhere. He switched on whatever equipment surrounded him and hoped for the best. The noises flooded to the far end of the house, and he plodded forward with the Beast out in front. He glanced down at the display in his hands. The screen showed a low battery icon. He'd forgotten to charge it earlier that afternoon.

"Damn!"

Nothing he could do about it now.

Something crashed more loudly upstairs, then thumped against the floor. The sound came from his room. Victor's room. He ran—no sense in creeping up on it—and a cold chill passed through him as he arrived at the top of the stairs. He shivered and hurried to get to his room before the disturbance escaped him again. Flipping on the light, he rushed into his room, hoping to catch the famed founder. Nothing visible with his eyes, but the Beast's display revealed a shifting, thin figure of blues and greens. The entity flipped his mattress upside down and tossed his possessions across the floor.

A moment later, the colors scattered, and the activity roared past him down the hallway. Each guest room door slammed shut along the way as the disturbance cascaded down the stairs.

Victor? It could only be him.

He hurried toward the noises again, checking the equipment he'd set up as he went. The infrared vision camera, the thermal camera, the audio recorder. All of them were operational. They must have recorded something. He grinned, and his heart quickened at the possibilities.

"Far too much drama for one day." If that was the kind of thing the previous tenants had dealt with, then no wonder they had all moved out. Only someone...

... crazy?...

... would choose to stay after such an occurrence.

More noises downstairs—stomping and pounding on doors. Then an explosion of shattering glass. He raced down the stairs with his pulse throbbing in his ears.

To think he could have missed all this excitement while wasting his time with Josie in the cemetery. All the action was happening *here*.

Stepping into the foyer with his Beast device up and ready, the noises stopped abruptly. His backup video camera and tripod lay broken on the floor over near the front door. Its lens was smashed, but that wasn't the worst of it. An entire wall of framed pictures in the entryway had dropped to the floor— thrown there?—and it sprinkled shards of glass in every direction. He was way past losing his deposit.

Between his gasping breaths, he stood still and tried to pinpoint the source of the disturbance. Nothing moved now, and he pivoted his head slowly, holding his breath and focusing on every creaking wall, every burst of air against the windows, and the rumbling of his stomach reminding him he hadn't eaten in hours.

All the drama had stopped.

He let out his breath and lowered his device. A moment later, footsteps raced up behind him.

Spinning around toward the noise, he instinctually braced for an impact. It came at him fast, and these weren't the same boots stomping this time, but some other entity. An aggressive spirit—he didn't need Emmie or Sarah to tell him that—whose icy presence chilled him to the bone as it passed through him. On its way out, it grabbed the back of his hair and twisted his head around with his body struggling to catch up. It thrust him backwards as he staggered to keep from toppling over, then whipped his head back and forth with his scalp on fire as his hair strained to stay intact.

Finn tried to face his attacker, to get some control over the situation, but it dragged him along toward the living room and forced him down to the floor until he stumbled onto his back. He was at its mercy now and he discarded his Beast device to defend himself. Swinging his fists through the unseen entity made no difference—he might as well have tried to battle a downpour of rain. Fighting it only strengthened its grip, threatening to tear out a major clump of his hair or even rip off a section of his scalp.

Scrambling backwards as it towed him closer to the base of a large oak bookcase, he hesitated to believe the truth until the bookcase started wobbling. The spirit intended to kill him. With his head still pinned to the floor, something pressed down against his neck. Fingers crept closer to his throat.

He stared up at the massive bookcase as it shuddered in place. It rocked forward and back, gaining momentum with each cycle, slamming again and again into the wall.

Within seconds, it was teetering above him at the tipping point. It could go either way now. He reached up and pushed against it. The thing must have weighed over a hundred pounds. Whatever unseen force loosening it from the wall had trapped him, and now it only had to finish the job. The bookcase crashed back against the wall one last time before breaking through the point of no return and tipped toward him. It would kill him now.

He scrambled to get out of the way, kicking his legs out first, then his torso and arms. The bookcase fell in slow motion. But he couldn't move his head—still caught in the grasp of his invisible executioner.

It'll crush my skull like a walnut.

Grabbing his Beast device from the floor next to him, he instinctually swung it up at the bookcase as if that might stop the thing from crashing down on him. The device sparked to life as it cracked against the side of the bookcase. The display flashed on and beeped.

In that moment, the entity's grasp on him disappeared. The chilly air rushed away, and the pressure was gone. Finn snapped his head sideways in the last second before the bookcase cracked against the wooden floor beside him. The house thundered from the impact.

He gasped.

Holy shit.

I'll never look at a bookcase the same way again. He stared wide-eyed at the ceiling until someone pounded on the front door.

Josie?

He staggered to his feet again and approached the door cautiously. Then it swung open before he reached it.

❧ 17 ❧

Emmie hurried up the steps to Caine House with Sarah beside her. But before they reached the door, it flew open and a rush of cold air burst out, hitting them like a wall of icicles. Emmie stumbled back and grabbed the handrail. Sarah lurched to the side as if struck by an unseen force.

Sarah shrieked, "Oh, my God!"

An icy chill whipped past them, escaping into the evening air as they recovered and stared inside through the open door. Finn was hunched over several feet back, with his hair in a mess as if he'd just climbed out of bed. One of his tripods, with the camera still attached to it, lay broken in the entryway and shattered glass littered the floor.

"Oh, thank God, you guys." He stumbled toward them with his shoes crunching over the glass.

They hurried over to him. The mess spread from wall to wall, and a bookcase lay on its side in the living room.

Emmie reached him first and lifted one of his arms. Sarah grabbed the other. "What happened to you?"

Finn looked dazed. "It's the most bizarre thing. This place is definitely haunted, and they sure don't like me."

"They did this?" Sarah gestured to the broken camera.

"I think..." Finn tried to straighten his hair. "... they were trying to kill me. I wasn't disturbing them or confronting them. Nothing like that, really. Just observing, but tonight I hit the paranormal jackpot, I guess."

"Lucky you."

They helped Finn across the foyer and gathered in the kitchen, as usual. Finn leaned against the counter and rubbed his head. "What a night."

"Let me see." Sarah examined his head and arms. "I don't see any bleeding. Did anything strike you?"

He glanced toward the living room. "Almost. I think I'll start wearing a helmet around the house, and maybe some elbow guards too. They were rough."

"How many were there?"

Finn shook his head. "I don't know. I guess just one tonight. That's all I saw on my devices this time."

Emmie folded her arms. "Some spirits are like that. At least, you didn't get cut or break any bones, right?"

"No bones. Just my dignity." Finn threw them a glance from the corner of his eyes. "But... what are you doing here? I mean, I'm happy you showed up when you did, but it's really late."

"This is important," Emmie said. "I've been trying to call you."

"I didn't have my phone with me where I was."

"Where were you?"

He formed an exasperated expression and winced while touching the back of his head. "Yeah, about that..."

"We were worried about you," Sarah said.

"How come?"

Emmie frowned. "You messed with that cross in the backyard crypt, didn't you?"

"Did I?" he asked in a small voice.

"Finn, it's really bad."

His voice got even smaller. "How bad?"

"That's why we're here. Your life's in danger. You know that box of belongings from my parents' car crash? I found an identical cross in there—same exact one—and I'm sure whatever caused their crash might come for you next."

"Damn, Emmie. I'm sorry..." Finn rubbed his forehead and groaned. "I think it found me. What is it, or they? Poltergeists?"

"We don't know yet."

Finn nodded. His eyes were bloodshot. "I *may* have bitten off more than I can chew here. I'm seriously questioning my choice of hobby. Listen, I'm a little rattled, and I hope this doesn't sound weird, but would you gals mind staying the night here, just to see what's happening?"

As Emmie turned to see if Sarah would be okay with it, her friend was already saying, "We wouldn't dream of leaving you alone."

He gave her a smile and a tender look. "I appreciate the protection. As you can see, the spirits are kicking my ass here."

"The guest rooms are clean, right?" Sarah asked.

"I think so. None of my junk in there, anyway, except for maybe a camera. I'll move it out."

"Sure you don't want to go back with us?" Emmie asked.

"I *did* rent this house for just this purpose," Finn said.

The broken glass lay scattered in every direction. "It could have been really bad, Finn. When did it start?"

"Well, it was quiet all day, but after I got back from the cemetery just now—"

"You went to the cemetery this late?"

"Yeah, I met this woman—"

"A woman?" Sarah's eyes widened.

Finn grimaced. "One of those New Age wannabe psychics, and I wanted to impress her."

Emmie laughed and stood, then went to the fridge. "Impress a woman by taking her to the cemetery? Now I understand why you're still single."

"I know it was a dumb idea... another dumb idea, but I guess I just wanted to prove to her that there wasn't anything to fear, and she went along with it. I see now she manipulated me into taking her there."

Sarah's eyes narrowed. "*She* manipulated *you* to go to the cemetery?"

"She was very... convincing."

There were only two beers in the fridge, but a bottle of wine on the counter beckoned to Emmie, and she took it. She didn't even mind that it didn't have a proper cork; less trouble to just twist it open, and less talk of *unscrewing* anything.

"Can I?" she asked.

"Absolutely," Finn said. "I'll join you."

She found wine glasses in a nearby cupboard and glanced back at Sarah as she pulled out three. "One for you?"

Sarah shook her head. "No, thanks." She turned to Finn. "So what's this girl's name?"

Finn rolled his eyes. "Josie."

Sarah nodded once. "Josie. Sounds sweet."

Finn shrugged. "Well..."

"Uh-oh, what happened?"

"It was going very well, at first, and we really clicked, until..."

Emmie poured the wine at the table. "She found out you hunt for ghosts?"

"Nope," Finn said. "Strangely enough, that wasn't the problem. She found that interesting, and that's how we ended up on a date in the cemetery."

Emmie laughed. "There's your first mistake."

Finn continued, "I know, but I thought I'd help her get over her fear of ghosts."

Sarah grinned. "So just like taking a girl to a horror movie, you thought she'd get all frightened and cozy up to you."

"That was the idea, and she was up for it, so... Why not? But here's when things went off the rails. She wanted me to pull out the cross from Victor Caine's grave, the same-looking cross as yours and the one in the crypt. I refused, and she ran off."

Setting the bottle on the table, Emmie stared at Finn. "And you think it's just a coincidence?"

"No," he said, "Obviously not. You have the same cross, it was in your parents' car, then I find one out back, and then this woman—"

"These crosses are artifacts from New Orleans. They are especially made to keep spirits in place."

"Oh, no," Finn groaned.

"Didn't you want spirits?" Emmie motioned around. "Looks like you got them."

"Didn't particularly want to free any." He took a big sip of wine and said, "I might as well tell you, and I meant to tell you before, that yes, I messed with the cross in the shed."

"You pulled it out?"

"It was more like an unscrewing. Please, no puns. My head hurts."

"That's the same kind as the one I found at home. Like a corkscrew below."

"That's it."

"But before I finished removing it I decided it wasn't a good idea and was going to put it back, but then it just sort of exploded and flew off, to the point where I thought it was booby-trapped or something. I was going to check that first, before I worried you."

"What else?" Emmie narrowed her eyes at him.

Finn glanced over toward the mess near the entryway and living room. "Some weird shit *did* happen today, especially after I got home from my date with Josie. It started off not too bad, with something whooshing by me, but then it got... worse. I brought the book with me to the cemetery..."

"Tell me you did not—"

"I did *not* read the book, I swear." He stopped with his hand over his heart and froze for a moment. "Josie asked me to take it to the cemetery."

Exchanging a glance with Emmie, Sarah said, "So she does know something about locking spirits."

"We have to find out more about it." Finn stood and paced a little. "This voodoo or whatever comes from New Orleans, but maybe it originated in France, and Josie is French..."

"If the cross stayed in Victor Caine's grave, then it might be safe to say none of the spirits is him," Sarah said.

"Oh," Finn said. "She also told me about Victor's cohort. Maybe you saw the ugly men in a painting over there? They committed suicide around the house and yard." He nodded meaningfully. "I thought the spirits here were Native Americans at first, like wanting revenge? But now that I know those guys killed themselves here, I'm pretty sure it's them. It would explain the boots and spurs."

Emmie turned to Sarah. "You feel anything?"

Sarah grinned a little grimly. "Just Finn's breaking heart. As for spirits, nothing."

"Would take more than this to break my heart," Finn said, and rubbed his hair. "Someone almost broke my head, though."

Emmie half closed her eyes in silence, then said, "Again, I don't see or feel any ghosts, although you know I don't see all adult spirits yet."

"Betty Wang told me I'd only see them if they want to be seen," he pointed out.

Emmie finished her glass of wine. That was another story. Betty Wang. But Finn sighed and looked exhausted, and Sarah was drooping too. They could continue in the morning.

"Let's get some sleep." Emmie stood and placed her glass near the sink. "We'll think better tomorrow, after some coffee."

"Don't say the word coffee," Finn mumbled in a gravelly voice. He rubbed the back of his head again and put away the wine. "Thank you for agreeing to stay the night. You can grab either room upstairs. Fully furnished."

Sarah stood and stepped over toward the foyer. Finn followed her. "I'll clean up the glass and everything tomorrow."

Emmie trailed them up the stairs. "Just try to get some sleep."

Settling into the guest room, Emmie kicked off her shoes and undressed, but left the bedside lamp on as she climbed under the sheets. Clean and fresh. Better than hotel sheets. Caine House wouldn't be so bad, if it weren't crawling with angry ghosts—and horrible wallpaper.

The echoes of Finn and Sarah moving in their rooms came through the door. She listened for any noises beyond the common squeaks and groans of an old house. Nothing. Whatever caused the disturbance to Finn earlier had escaped when they arrived. Would it come back?

And had the same spirit or spirits killed her parents?

Too much to think about now. She had survived growing up in terror with the Hanging Girl, and she would survive this, and so would her friends.

Emmie closed her eyes and allowed the wine's comforting warmth to lull her to sleep.

The next morning, there were still no signs of the disturbance Finn had encountered. But where had the ghosts gone? Except for the footsteps in the hallway and downstairs belonging to Finn and Sarah, Emmie enjoyed the silence after having slept quite well.

Maybe the nightmares and the thoughts of her parents would catch up with her, but she climbed out of bed with energy and slipped on the clothes she'd worn the previous day.

Someone had already cleaned the mess in the foyer, and Emmie found them in the kitchen. Finn was making toast while Sarah sat at the kitchen table with a big grin. Sarah motioned for her to come over.

"I would have helped." Emmie crossed the kitchen toward Sarah.

"I know." Finn's back was turned toward her. "That's why I let you two sleep."

Emmie sat down beside Sarah. They had set the table for breakfast too, with glasses of orange juice, bacon, and scrambled eggs on the plate already.

"So you can cook?" Emmie smiled.

"Well, I *am* single, after all. I can take care of myself. It's easy enough to throw a pizza in the oven and clean up my messes, and I even keep my laundry colors from fading. I'm a jack-of-all-trades, you know."

"I see that."

"If I had pancake mix, I could whip up some, but..."

"I've always wanted to stay in a bed-and-breakfast," Sarah said. The French occult book was sitting beside her plate.

Emmie gestured to it. "Were you reading that?"

Sarah picked it up and passed it to Emmie. "No, I understand almost nothing. Just curious."

While eating some of the breakfast, Emmie flipped through the book and read some of the passages, or rather a word here and there, although not out loud. "I'm proud of you, Finn."

"The food?"

"No, I'm proud that you didn't read any of the passages. I shouldn't have given to you in the first place, but I didn't think about it. Good thing you resisted when your lady friend was pressuring you to take the cross, too."

"I learned my lesson after the first one almost blew my hand off, so I wasn't about to try that again, not even for a hot redhead."

"The book is connected to that cross, though, and she knew it. Maybe we can stop by the cemetery sometime and check out Victor's grave. I'm not sure what we're looking for, but..." Emmie closed the book and pressed her palm over the cover. "I guess we should keep this in a safe place."

"Did your parents speak French?" Sarah asked.

"No. At least, I don't think so. But they could have translated a few passages and memorized them."

"Have you ever been over to the accident site?" Sarah asked after a moment.

"No." Emmie stared down at the book. "I never brought myself to do it before. And now, here I am. Only about a mile away from it, but..." Her voice trailed off.

Sarah rubbed Emmie's back. "If you ever decide to go there, I would go with you."

Emmie nodded. "Thank you."

Without making any comment, Finn carried over the plates of toast and passed them out before sitting across from them.

"Well, I'm afraid I have an ulterior motive for making you this banquet."

"I wouldn't call it a banquet."

"Jeez, Emmie, I bet you never leave five stars for anything."

Sarah laughed. "She's a total three-to-one star lady, with the occasional four and the very rare five."

"What is it, Finn?"

"It's not that bad." Finn held up a hand. "I'm just wondering if you wouldn't mind staying here for another night or two... or three. I mean, last night wasn't too crazy, right? Well, not *after* you arrived." He rubbed the back of his head. "Something's gone off the rails here—too many coincidences—and we haven't gotten to the bottom of it, and I just think last night wasn't a good representation of what I've experienced when you've been gone. It's almost like the ghosts are avoiding you."

"How do you feel about that?" Sarah asked Emmie.

"I have to face what happened," Emmie said. "And all this is leading me to it. But what about you? You haven't been feeling well, and I think this is big, Sarah."

"True." Finn looked at Sarah as well.

Sarah took her time answering, biting off a piece of toast with a pensive expression. "I suppose we could stay. I *am* on vacation after all. As long as this bed-and-breakfast thing continues..."

Finn smiled. "It will."

"Okay." Sarah ate another bite of food, although Emmie still watched her.

"Sure." Emmie nodded. "We need to see this through, for your sake and now mine, too, Finn."

The floor rumbled, interrupting her; the noise was coming

from somewhere in the next room. Finn stopped and listened, turning in his chair toward the sound. *"That's* the furnace kicking in. I've already checked it out."

Emmie flipped through the French book again as she ate. One page opened faster than the others, and she found a small pink bookmark stuck inside. She pulled it out and examined it. She recognized the handwriting first. It was a folded school art project she'd made for her mother as a child. A Mother's Day gift —funny that she remembered creating it after all those years. Just a drawing of a red rose with the words "Happy Mother's Day" below it. A bittersweet memory, knowing that it had been with her parents during the accident.

"What's that?" Sarah asked.

"Looks like my parents marked a section." Emmie returned the bookmark. "Finn, I'll need your help with this."

❧ 19 ❦

After breakfast, Emmie drove Sarah back home to prepare for their stay at Caine House. Even though Hanging House was less than an hour away, they packed two small suitcases, filling it with supplies they'd need to stay with Finn for a couple of nights, and informed Alice Hyde that she would have the home to herself while they were gone. Alice's mood changed from gloomy to cheerful after hearing the news, but she also made Sarah promise to make up for the lost time by playing the piano songs twice when she returned.

In the afternoon they headed back, driving through the picturesque town of Lake Eden and then following the same winding gravel roads toward Caine House. Turning right at the crossroads past the cemetery, Emmie couldn't help but think about the place where her parents had died. *Not too far away. Just straight ahead over that hill and around a sharp corner.* She had looked up the location on an Internet map, zooming into the spot, somehow expecting to see her parents' spirits standing next to the tree where they had died.

She could go there now—she had time—but instead pushed the thought away and continued along the gravel road to the house with their suitcases rattling in the backseat.

"I hope Finn has managed to translate the part of the book that was marked," Sarah said. "That must be an important ceremony or something."

"He'll do what we would do, type it into an Internet translation page. At least with whatever French he knows he'll be able to tell whether the translation is good."

"Or he can call that New Age girl of his." Sarah scoffed.

Emmie laughed. "I worry about him."

"I can't believe he took her to the cemetery at night for a first date."

"His idea of romance, I guess."

Sarah shook her head and looked over with a wide grin. "*Maybe* a second date."

They laughed together.

The sun glared off the windshield, and Emmie flipped down the sun visor to keep her eyes on the road. Something up ahead caught her eye. Standing off near an open section of the cornfield to the right, Emmie spotted a boy, about twelve years old, dressed in clothes that would have been worn by someone over a hundred years earlier: a white, long-sleeved shirt and muddy brown trousers with suspenders. He had short black hair and stood barefoot in the black soil without an expression as they approached.

"Oh no," Emmie said.

Sarah looked over at her. "What's wrong?"

"I think I've seen our first ghost here." Emmie gestured toward the boy. "Do you feel anything?"

Emmie slowed the car and moved it to the side of the road.

Sarah's eyelids drooped as she stared ahead, still watching the road. "I feel fear. Is it a boy over there?"

"Yes."

Pulling the car over along the shoulder, Emmie let her right tires catch the edge of the ditch. She parked and they climbed out into the partly cloudy afternoon air.

Caine House was just a couple hundred feet farther, but it could wait a little longer.

Emmie approached the boy, although he backed away a few steps before disappearing into the stalks of corn. Within the rows, she still spotted his ragged clothes.

"Don't be afraid. What's your name?"

The boy didn't answer, but he didn't run either. He only stared at her while she approached him cautiously, as if attempting to tame some wild animal. The child victims tended to come to her willingly, but something was disturbing this boy even more than usual.

She looked for any signs of injury that might help explain why he was alone, out near a country road like that. There were no cemeteries nearby, and no obvious signs of trauma on his body. But sometimes a spirit had a different reason to attach itself to a location, aside from suicide or murder. Over the years she had learned that sometimes a spirit just lost its way after being released from this world or became attached to something it had left behind. Maybe this boy was waiting for his parents to come home and find him, or maybe he was guarding some other secret.

"You don't have to be afraid. Come here and tell me what happened to you."

The boy inched forward but showed no sign that he was truly interested in talking with her. Without a word, he slipped his hands into his pockets and looked over his shoulders every few seconds, as if someone were about to catch him.

"Are you hiding? Who are you hiding from? Are you in trouble with your parents?"

The boy looked around, then drew in his arms and hunched down. He shivered as if freezing.

"Do you want us to help you?" Emmie stepped forward again, and the boy leaned back. "You can understand me, right?"

He nodded.

"That's good. We can talk if you want to. What's your name? My name is Emmie."

The boy opened his mouth as if he would speak at that moment, but he ducked suddenly, throwing his arms over his head and crouching into a ball. He moaned as if about to get attacked.

Tense, his head whipping from side to side, he kept his eyes wide. He whimpered, then turned sideways, staring at her over his shoulder.

She held out her hand to him. "Stay with me. I can help you if you want. Please tell me your name."

"David," he said.

"Okay, David. Tell me what happened."

The boy gasped as he turned his back to her moments before he ran away.

"Wait, David. Don't go."

A red spot appeared on the back of his shirt, still bleeding and draining down like a fresh wound. Emmie recognized this moment. It was the end of the eternal looping tragedy that consumed the boy's existence now, the last actions of his life, when someone had cut him down, throwing him into that unending broken record. David darted into the cornfield before Emmie could get any closer.

"He's terrified," Sarah said.

"He's running away. I'll have to wait until I see him later. This one might take a while."

They got back in the car and continued to Caine House.

Pulling into the driveway, Sarah growled, "Now I feel something different."

"What?"

"A dark energy, like... *murderous.*"

"That doesn't sound good." Emmie looked up at one of the front upstairs windows. The shadow of a figure moved behind the glass. At first she assumed it was Finn, until he appeared in the doorway below.

As Emmie turned off the engine and climbed out of the car, Finn hurried to them. He wasn't smiling.

"Uh-oh." Sarah climbed out and called, "What's wrong?"

Finn didn't answer until he reached them. "Remember that Betty woman I told you about? She's in our backyard."

20

By the time they circled around the house, Betty was there, and looking more like the woman Emmie remembered. She was older and seemed even smaller, and instead of the slacks and cardigans of a librarian she wore a long dress that stretched down to her brown suede boots, and gemstones around her neck. She was also clutching a handful of grass and earth, her eyes closed as if she were drawing strength from nature itself.

They approached her slowly. Betty stretched out her arms as if embracing the sky.

Sarah whispered, "What is she doing?"

As Emmie stepped closer, an odd smell, like spicy incense, hung in the air around her. A familiar scent from long ago. "Excuse me, can we help you?"

Betty turned around. Her face was buried in wrinkles, but she had the same intense look in her eyes that Emmie remembered.

"Betty?" Finn asked. "Do you need something?"

"Not yet." Betty closed her eyes and turned to the side, as if adjusting herself like a satellite dish to get the best signal. "But something has changed. The energy is dark, and it's not safe.

You've seen something strange in there, haven't you? Something very unusual."

"Yes. A lot of paranormal activity. The ghosts found me, like you said."

"That's not the disturbance I'm referring to. The spirits that have haunted the halls of Caine House have gone silent, and something worse has moved inside. It's not safe for you to stay here." She walked closer to the crypt.

"Are you a psychic?" Emmie asked.

Betty ignored the question. "Have you seen any ghosts in this area? Near this crypt?"

"No, I can't see spirits," Finn said.

Betty looked directly at Emmie. "What about you, Emmie Fisher? Have you seen or felt anything around this house?"

Emmie stared at her for a moment. "So I do know you. It *was* you."

"I supposed you might remember me. I knew your parents. I knew them well."

"Who are you?" Emmie asked, walking toward her.

"We should have a talk soon. I can explain a few things about your past, but first I need to know why this house has become a beacon of darkness, a heaviness like I haven't encountered in a long time."

"Is that why you stopped by?" Finn asked.

"Everything leads back to this house," Betty said, while stepping over to the crypt. "I need to go in there and see her grave."

"I went in there," Finn said.

Betty stopped and stiffened, then turned her head back toward him. "Did you disturb the grave?"

Finn met Emmie's gaze before answering. "I started unscrewing the cross—"

The old woman fully turned. "After I told you not to mess with anything that was fixed?"

"I had already done it."

"Ah!" she cried in frustration, clenching her fists. "I knew you were a fool."

"Whoa, lady!" Finn cried.

Betty's voice rose above Finn's. "The grave contained the spirit of a very powerful woman. A spirit I shouldn't have to deal with at my age. Did you see a spirit?"

Finn hesitated. "No. I mean, I did see a flash of light on the recording."

Betty frowned and calmed a bit, then turned to Emmie. "Can you still see spirits, Emmie? You haven't suppressed your gift, have you?"

Emmie's chest tightened. "I'm still psychic, if that's what you mean, but I wouldn't call it a gift."

"Don't be a ninny. I told your parents they had to be stronger with you. Throw you into the deep end. All this pussyfooting about only leads to this."

"Pussyfooting? I was a child, seeing ghosts everywhere."

"And you'll always see them. Get over it. They should have helped you hone your powers. You are one in a generation."

"They didn't help me," Emmie said angrily. "And they died doing something crazy here."

"They died doing what was right, but they didn't have your gift. You need to understand your responsibility, Emmie. Maybe you will now." Betty began pulling her sleeves up as if she were about to enter a physical fight.

"Is it your fault they're dead?" Emmie trembled and held back a deeper rage until she felt a hand close around hers and squeeze it. Sarah was by her side. "You came to live in this town after they died, didn't you?"

"To put things right. And now I have to do it again." Betty shook her head, then stared at the crypt. "I'm afraid we don't have time to discuss anything now—but soon. A great danger has surrounded us."

She indicated the door with her head, and Finn stepped

toward the crypt, digging inside his pocket. He pulled out the key and unlocked the door.

"I pray the worst hasn't happened," Betty said grimly before walking in.

"What's the worst?" Finn whispered.

They entered the crypt after the old woman, circling the cement slab. She was staring at the black cross that still lay beside the head of the grave.

Betty groaned and shook her head again. "She escaped. Oh, she is out!"

21

"I knew this might happen since you removed the cross!" Betty scowled at Finn.

"I tried to put it back," Finn said, stepping around the camera equipment he'd left in there earlier. "But it had broken from the grave. It even flew off before I finished unscrewing it."

"I said she is powerful. Very." Betty's eyes widened. "And that was the moment you saw the flash of light you mentioned?"

Finn swallowed. "Yes."

"I don't sense anyone's presence..." Sarah said softly.

Betty's sharp eyes darted to her, and she tilted her head, examining Sarah. "So you are another. Do you see ghosts or just feel them?"

For a second, Sarah looked startled. "I feel them. Hear them, sometimes."

Nodding, Betty asked. "Feel their pain, their anger?"

"Yes." Sarah blinked and stared back at Betty.

"Takes it out of you, huh?"

"How do you know?"

"You're what we call an empath." Betty nodded again. "You can be useful,"—she looked from her to Emmie, pointing first at one, then at the other—"and you two together can be dangerous.

Like a chemical reaction. If you learn to use the combination, it's gold, but green as you are, it can help the other side instead." Her eyes narrowed, and she leaned into Sarah. "Your parents should have forced you, like mine did."

"I think you're scaring her," Finn said a little more firmly, moving forward.

Emmie looked down at the grave. "Why don't you tell us what you know of this spirit."

Betty pursed her lips and stepped toward the cross now. "She was a psychic of exceptional ability. She should have helped others, fought against evil, but instead she got intoxicated by her own power. She was a very beautiful woman, and that was perhaps her undoing. Sometimes beauty is a curse."

"Don't I know it." Finn grinned and nodded.

Emmie rolled her eyes. "Not the time."

"Sorry, what was her name?" Finn asked faintly.

"Josephine Burdette."

"Oh, shit."

The three women stared at Finn.

Betty asked sharply, "Did you see someone like that?"

"Do you mean *Josie?*" Emmie mumbled.

"Cemetery girl?" Sarah said.

Finn's expression showed his confusion. "That sounds hard to believe. She was flesh and blood," he told Betty. "I can assure you. This wasn't some ghost..."

Betty raised her hand. "What did she look like?"

Finn's eyes angled up to the side, and he grinned a little. "Long red hair, blue eyes—yeah, I'd say kind of beautiful."

"What was she wearing?"

He shrugged. "What difference—? All right, a dress, a white dress. Like boho, New Age, I don't know."

Betty scoffed. "Early twentieth century, more like. Ghosts can't really change clothes, can they?"

"I don't know," Finn repeated. "But fashion is all over the place now, how could I know—"

"Jewelry?" Betty pursued.

Finn thought about it. "She wore a few necklaces, I remember, one with a turquoise stone in it."

"In the shape of two concentric circles?"

"Yeah, that's it."

"And what did she want with you? Did she want to stay in the house?"

"No. She told me some stuff about the ghosts, and I convinced her to go with me to Caine's grave last night."

"You didn't convince her," Betty said grimly. "She tricked you. Josephine was a master at deception, and the cemetery is where she needed you, so she took you there."

"What for?"

"Revenge, a disease that doesn't stop with physical death. Josephine's disease has eaten away at her for a long time. She's been in here a century, roiling inside in neither heaven, hell, or purgatory, straining and fretting to get out. She could cause a tide of evil to overcome Lake Eden and spread much further."

"Look," Finn said with some energy, "I wasn't looking at some spirit or illusion or anything like that. This was a real woman, a physical woman, not anything like a ghost."

"I'm sure it was her."

Emmie jumped into the conversation. "How could Finn see this woman as solid and interact with her? Is he a psychic too?"

The old woman eyed Finn from head to toe. "I doubt it." Then she turned back to Emmie and continued, "I told you. The combination of you two." Betty glanced from Emmie to Sarah once more. "That's what made it possible. When certain psychic powers meet, they can complement each other, creating an even greater energy, and energy is what Josephine thrives on. You were here, together, before she appeared to him, yes?"

Sarah nodded with wide eyes. "Yes."

"Then there you go. All she needed to do was will your friend to see her. All ghosts in the house, all that are around the two of you, can manifest this way now, if they wish to. Together, you magnify the physical."

Emmie considered the concept, and one person came to mind. "The Hanging Girl..."

Betty nodded. "That was the spirit in the house where you lived. She became physical now?"

"Not to others, but she physically hurt me recently. She could never do that in all the years I grew up in that house. That's because of Sarah?"

"Yes, and others will take advantage of your combined energy in the future, so you should both learn to defend yourself against evil, which is why, Emmie Fisher, your parents worked so hard to train you. They sought to protect and strengthen you against the dangers they knew you would face."

A wave of mixed feelings swept through Emmie. This revelation was too confusing for that moment, or for it to dispel the bitterness she'd felt for so long, even if it had been motivated by love. The untangling of so many emotions would take time—something they didn't have now.

Sarah spoke up. "I don't see the Hanging Girl at all."

"That's to be expected. She doesn't want you to see her. If she were a powerful psychic, such as Josephine, then she *would* become visible even to those who normally cannot see spirits, like Finn. Josephine has powers far beyond your own and maybe even beyond mine. Still, we have to bring her back and lock her into this grave where she belongs."

"She wanted the cross from Victor Caine's grave," Finn said. "She kept talking about a man having to be careful if he loved her, and kept singing about it, in fact."

"Oh, yes. Hell hath no fury like a psychic scorned."

"What did Victor do?" Finn asked.

"I just said. Scorned her." Betty looked at the cross, her eyes lost. "Betrayed her. She cannot remove that cross alone, as she is a spirit, and cursed by him. That is why she came to entice you."

Finn folded his arms over his chest. "Well, it didn't work. Can she do the same to some other guy?"

"Yes, and a whole lot of other things, if she succeeds..." Betty faced them. "No time to lose. We'll have a long talk afterwards, but before all that, we have to find Josephine. I need your help. Everyone should focus." She looked at Emmie. "I'm sure your parents advised you on how to do this if they followed my advice? Do you remember the steps to call a spirit to you?"

"I'll never forget," Emmie said. "Meditate and communicate."

"That's correct. Your parents said you could do it when you were young, although I'm sure it wasn't the most pleasant thing. Unfortunately, the new spirit in this house is not a pleasant person."

"That's an understatement." Finn scoffed. "And she has it in for me."

Betty turned to Sarah. "Have you ever focused on bringing a spirit to you?"

"I've never tried."

"I know your strength is your connection with emotions. I sense a great sadness within you now, but I need you to focus like they trained Emmie to do. Meditate and focus on the spirit, the hollowness that you feel here. An absence can be like a presence for someone like you. Then communicate the message that she *must* appear before us. Between the three of us, we can force Josephine back here, and once she's in our midst, just leave things to me. Your job will be to focus so much that she can't escape. Can you do that?"

Emmie and Sarah nodded and moved closer to Betty.

"Don't you need that French book?" Finn asked. "This morning, I found the part that I think locks the spirits back into the grave. 'At each turn,' it says, and I think it means at each turn of the cross being screwed in."

Betty had closed her eyes, and she opened one to glare at Finn. "A little clever, like I said. And a bit too late. But I know the ceremony and the words by heart, my boy. I told you, I've lived for a long time and done this before."

Emmie glanced over at Finn. He had switched on the thermal camera attached to the tripod, while taking a position behind it with one hand guiding its aim. Always in research mode, that guy—never missing a chance to record something like what might be about to happen. His Beast device sat at his feet like some weapon he might use in battle.

The old woman gestured toward Josephine's grave. "I think it would be best if we all gather around, one on each side. That way we can bring her back to the exact spot where I want her."

But the door to the crypt slammed shut, and the room went dark.

Finn gasped near the doorway.

"Open the door, Finn!" Emmie cried.

"Not me! I didn't do that."

Emmie scrambled to pull her cellphone from her pocket, but Finn's cellphone lit up the area first. A woman stood in the room with them.

"Josie," Finn said.

22

E mmie looked up to meet the woman they were meant to fear, and she seemed more beautiful than anything Finn had described. No wonder he had fallen head over heels for her.

Josephine's blue eyes were entrancing, matching her turquoise necklace and radiating in the darkness. Her white dress stood out, and her long red hair flowed down over her shoulders, some of it brushing across her exposed cleavage.

"Hello, Finn," she said in a low, seductive voice. "It's so wonderful to see you again, although we didn't part on the best of terms. But I figured you wouldn't mind being left alone there among the dead."

Finn aimed the thermal camera on the tripod toward her as his gaze jumped between her and the device's screen. "I don't believe it..."

"What don't you believe? That I am so beautiful? That an angel stands before you? You flatter me."

Emmie glimpsed Finn's display. Purple and blue shapes defined Josephine's form.

"Josephine," Betty said, "let go of your lust for revenge and accept your fate or we'll return you to your grave."

"Have we met, *ma vieille*?" Josephine stared at Betty with a sneer. "Why don't you take my place, already? Not much life left in you."

"Betty?" Emmie said.

"Just do your thing." The old woman drew herself up and clenched her fists. "Sarah, you can feel her energy, so do as we said once I begin the process."

Josephine stood before them, seeming as real as anybody else. All the other spirits Emmie had encountered were not flesh and blood like this woman; everyone could see her. By the look on Finn's face, he was struggling to accept that the woman he'd taken to the cemetery was not only an imposter, but not alive.

Once more, Betty closed her eyes and stretched out her arms toward Josephine as if to give her a hug.

Josephine cringed as something yanked her forward a few inches. "Don't bother, old woman. You're just getting in my way. I have work to do."

"I can't let you succeed," Betty said calmly but sternly, as if talking to a child. "The damage—"

"You want to talk about damage? Consider what he did to me."

"I won't defend him, but there's no room for your vengeance in this town. You need to let go of what happened and move on in peace, or it will send you to a worse existence."

"He will receive what he deserves, and nothing's going to stop me."

"You are arrogant. There are powers greater than you." Betty tensed, now staring at Josephine through narrow eyes. "You won't escape your grave if you don't let go."

Josephine groaned as she twisted within Betty's unseen grasp. "You can't control me. I'm stronger. You might have been powerful at some point in your life, but your mind is clouded now. Nothing but weakness remains."

She suddenly turned toward Sarah. "An empath—ineffective against me. And you." She looked at Emmie. "How can you stop me? You're half the strength of that old woman." Her eyes slid to Finn. "And my boyfriend doesn't have a clue." She laughed.

"I figured you out, eventually." Finn's face turned red.

"You are a proud boy, Finn," she pursued. "Why have you hidden your floods of tears for your dead brother from your friends here and everyone else, *mon bel homme*? You call me vain, but that is vanity. Do you fear being seen as weak? Do you fear them questioning your failures? Why did Neil blow his brains out, *mon chéri*? Why didn't you know he was going to do it?"

Finn didn't answer, but he had stepped away from his thermal camera.

Josephine moved closer to Betty now and reached for her throat. "I will end this now."

Betty stepped back, raised her hands, and Josephine froze.

Emmie continued to focus on Josephine to keep her from escaping. All she could do was hope that Betty had a strategy in mind. Josephine wasn't easy to hold. Her spirit vibrated with dark energy, and it pulled at Emmie's mind. She hadn't used her gift to influence a spirit in that way before, just to summon them. But now the focus on Josephine yanked at Emmie's mind, and it hurt.

What had her parents taught her? What were the words or actions that might keep a spirit away? With the Hanging Girl, Emmie could distract the spirit, get it to focus on something other than its obsession. Emmie commented on the only thing she saw about Josephine that might work.

"Your necklace is beautiful. Did your mother give it to you?"

Josephine glanced over at her. "It's none of your—" She stiffened as Betty motioned her in closer.

"That's good, Emmie," Betty said. "You've done this before."

Josephine's body twisted and strained as she backed a step. "You're wasting my time. You won't get me that easily." She thrust herself away from them.

Emmie continued, "Is it a gift from someone you loved?"

"So your power is to bore me to death? Your skills are nothing against me. Whoever taught you failed miserably."

The image of Emmie's parents came into her mind. The pressure and frustration returned as she fought to remember their training. They had taught her as best they could for just such an encounter, and now she regretted having fought their instructions over the years. She wished she'd listened a little better when she'd had the chance. It might be too late; Josephine might be right.

"Did Victor Caine give it to you?" Emmie cried out.

A long, furious shriek escaped Josephine, though it seemed as though she could not move. Finn was recording her again, although now he was using his Beast device. His forehead glistened with sweat in the glare from the device's screen.

The muscles in Betty's face and neck tightened. "It is working."

Sarah moved closer to Josephine, reaching out as Betty was doing.

Josephine twisted, then turned back to Finn, who was still aiming his camera at her. Her voice changed, now soft and sweet. "Finn, don't let them do this to me. *Il faut que tu m'aides.* You swore you would help me."

"No can do," he said, staring at her through the screen.

Betty was within an arm's length of Josephine. She could have reached out and grabbed her at that point, but Emmie was sure that's not how it worked. The old woman shuddered almost to the point of convulsions as she dragged Josephine down without touching her, closer to the ground and toward the cross.

Sarah also strained while reaching out and touching Josephine's shoulder.

Josephine railed against the domination. Her physical presence faded, revealing the familiar shadowy form that Emmie had seen so many times in her life. The form shifted slowly as Josephine struggled to hang onto the physical. With Betty pulling her toward the grave and Sarah pushing her from her physical manifestation, she lashed out and swung her arms through Betty's body.

Betty stumbled backwards and cried out with her hand over her heart.

Josephine brightened and took another swipe at Betty, this time thrusting her arms through her throat. "You won't survive."

Gasping for breath, the old woman collapsed. Her eyes widened and locked with Josephine's.

"No!" Sarah stretched out her hand toward Betty.

Emmie reached Betty first and held the old woman upright while struggling to control the situation. "Don't stop!" she begged Sarah. "Concentrate."

Josephine spoke to Sarah. "You can't force someone to go who doesn't want to. Not with *your* pathetic skills. Don't you know that?"

Emmie softly shook the old psychic. "Betty?"

With a hand that trembled, Betty managed to reach into her pocket and pull out something in her clenched fist. She passed it to Emmie, pressing it into her palm with wavering strength. "Use it."

Emmie glanced at it. A key.

Betty's lips quivered as if to say something important, but it was lost as her last breath escaped her mouth instead. Her eyes rolled up, and her body went limp.

A chill swept through Emmie. Not from a vile spirit passing, but from the realization that a thousand answers and possibly the last connection to her parents had disappeared forever. A moment later, a warm presence embraced Emmie, starting around her chest and moving up through her face. The warmth formed the vague outline of the old woman before scattering into the darkness. "Betty just died!"

Sarah gasped.

Emmie glared at Josephine. "You killed her?"

"The same will happen to you if you get in my way," Josephine said with abandon, as if she had just grown stronger.

Finn stepped forward between them, reaching out toward Josephine as if to grab her himself. His hands passed through her, but she shuddered as the Beast device he was carrying went through her spirit.

Josephine moved toward Finn. "I'll snatch your soul and drag it at my side, *mon chéri*. You wanted to be with me. As you see, it's not so difficult."

Sarah pushed past Finn and embraced Josephine's spirit. A flash of light burst where Josephine stood, and she disappeared as Sarah dropped to the ground.

Emmie screamed and left Betty to jump to her friend's side. "Sarah!"

Finn put the Beast on the slab and kneeled by her. "Are you okay?"

As he propped up Sarah and moved the hair away from her face, Emmie scanned the area for any sign of Josephine. She was gone. Had they accomplished what Betty had attempted and captured her? Or had Sarah released her soul?

Sarah moaned. She rolled to the side and then sat up with Finn's arm around her back. Struggling to stay upright, she looked around. "We got her."

Emmie nodded. "*You* got her."

"All of us." Sarah touched her chest. "But that felt strange."

"In what way?" Finn asked. "She passed on. She's gone. We saw it."

"I don't know. It wasn't the same."

While Emmie helped Sarah, Finn stood and scanned the room with his device. "Nothing on the screen. She's gone. Did you put her back in her grave?"

"I don't think so," Sarah said faintly.

"I would know if she was still here," Emmie said. "Sarah, do you feel her?"

Sarah nursed her arm. "No."

Emmie nodded. "We must have done it together, like Betty said. We're a dangerous combination, remember?"

Sarah nodded with a subtle smile.

"Can you stand?" Finn asked, bending down to take her hand.

Sarah nodded, and they helped her stand up, each grabbing an arm.

Now Emmie focused her cellphone's light down on Betty's serene face. "We need to call 911."

※ 23 ※

They had taken Betty outside and locked the crypt after calling 911. Sarah had tried to revive her unsuccessfully on the grass, and the late afternoon breeze blew peacefully through their hair as they took turns doing chest compressions on the old woman, as Sarah instructed them, until the first police car arrived and an officer took over. Even before the officer's stunned expression after seeing the old woman lying motionless on the ground, Emmie knew the truth—Betty was gone.

Before long, two more police cars arrived, and an ambulance, and then lots of questions. Emmie stayed by Sarah's side as Finn took the lead in explaining what had happened, using his newly regained ability to lie under pressure. No talk of the crypt or ghosts or any psychic phenomena.

When they questioned Emmie, it brought back all the memories of when she was a child answering questions for police chief John Ratner and the other investigators back at the Hanging House. John would most likely hear about the incident, and she heeded the advice he'd given her long ago: Tell the truth, but keep it simple.

The investigation went smoothly, and she never felt they suspected foul play. She had dropped in the lawn, the three of them said, and they had tried to revive her. Sarah's status as a hospital nurse added another layer of credibility, and the incident passed without any drama. One of the officers had even known Betty as the retired librarian, and since she was a woman in her early eighties, he commented that having a stroke at her age wasn't unlikely.

Still, they were all shaken by Betty's death. Sarah cried after she was done talking with a large woman police officer, who was a little puzzled as to why she felt so strongly about Betty so soon after just meeting her. Emmie discreetly mentioned Sarah's loss to the officer, and they stopped asking questions.

They hadn't known Betty well, but she had stepped up to protect them. Confronting Josephine was difficult enough without having to deal with the police and the ambulance taking the body away.

The entire process took a couple of hours, and eventually they were left alone.

"I'm sorry, you guys," Finn said as they sat, too tired even to get anything to drink or eat. "I feel like this is my fault."

They had gathered in the living room this time, with Sarah sprawled out on the couch. Emmie sat in an antique chair across from Finn, who occupied a rocking chair. He rocked back and forth for a few minutes, stopped to run his hands over his face and through his hair, then continued rocking.

"What, Finn?" Emmie asked.

Finn groaned. "I kissed her."

"A *French* kiss?" Emmie cringed at her own bad joke and then let out an almost hysterical laugh.

"Is there another kind?" Finn rolled his eyes.

This brought a smile to Sarah's face for the first time that day. "That is so disgusting."

"Don't ask me anything else," he begged.

"We don't want to know." Emmie laughed again. "That *thing* might have even fooled me too if I had confronted her in an everyday situation."

Finn furrowed his brow and looked around the area. "Could she still be here in the house with us?"

"I didn't feel her spirit leave," Sarah said. "She just went away."

"What's the difference?" Finn asked. "I mean, the nuance?"

"Can't explain," Sarah said.

"There's a lot I don't know about this stuff, despite all the experiences in my life, so imagine Sarah, who is new to this." Emmie glanced around some more. "I don't see her anywhere, but she could just be hiding until after we leave." She looked at Finn. "Maybe she intends to manipulate you again."

Finn pressed his eyes closed for a moment. "At least I didn't do what she asked me to, or maybe things would be a lot worse than they are. I mean, what do you think would have happened if I had removed Victor's cross?"

A sadness passed through Emmie. No more simple answers. "That would be a question for Betty. And unfortunately, she's not here anymore to help us. We've got to be careful now because if Josephine is still here, then she knows who we are and our strengths." She looked at Finn. "She seems to know our weaknesses too, and she'll use them."

Finn stared at the floor. "Looks like she even knows stuff we never told her..."

Emmie understood, but stayed silent. The mystery of Finn's obsession with ghosts, at least, was solved. His brother had killed himself, and from what Josephine had implied, Finn didn't know why. Emmie leaned her head back on the chair, sorry to see the pain on his face. All the bravado, the humor, hiding so much sorrow. She glanced at Sarah, who seemed to be suffering with Finn now; Sarah had to learn not to do that too much.

Emmie closed her eyes and replayed the events before Betty's death in her mind. She and Sarah had focused their energies on Josephine, but Finn had aimed the device in his hand at her as if it were a weapon.

"When we were all trying to control Josephine, what was

happening on that device of yours?" she asked him. "Were you recording it?"

Finn paused before answering. "Yes, but Josephine's data looked like anyone else's. Human."

"But I remember you looked surprised."

Finn straightened up a little. "I was, but I'm not sure the device was working correctly. It was a little odd. When I focused the electromagnetic radiation to pulse from the Beast, blasting out the energy rather than just receiving it, it appeared I got a reaction from her. Not a lot, but when I aimed it at her, she moved out of the way. But I doubt we will put spirits in their graves by irritating them."

"Still, they are a form of energy, so maybe your devices are messing with that?"

Before he could reply, Sarah turned on the couch, her face toward the ceiling. She was pale, as if she would throw up at any moment. She sat up before trying to stand and wobbled, grabbing the arm of the couch until Finn jumped up and helped her.

"You don't look so good," he said. "Maybe just get some rest."

She nodded and looked at him. "I will."

"How about some water?"

"Coffee?"

"Of course. Coffee. Coming up." Finn stepped into the kitchen.

Emmie put her arm around Sarah's back. "Do you want to see a doctor?"

Sarah shook her head.

"Maybe just take it easy for a while. You've been through a lot lately. I'm sorry you had to witness what Betty suffered, especially after what happened to your grandmother."

Sarah looked straight ahead and clutched her hands together. "I tried everything I could to follow her instructions. I pushed as hard as I could to help, but Josephine just wouldn't go."

"But she did. We couldn't have done it without you. And I can see I need to train myself now, continue with the things my parents were trying to teach me. I never want this sort of thing to happen ever again."

"How are we going to stop Josephine if she comes back?"

Emmie nodded. "We'll figure that out, but for now, you should go back home, Sarah. I think that might be the best thing to do."

"But what will you do if she shows up again and I'm gone? You need me here. I can still help." She sat straighter. "I'm not feeling that bad. I won't leave."

Brushing a strand of purple hair behind her friend's ear, Emmie said, "Okay, but then at least go upstairs and try to get some rest. I swear, one of us will scream if we run into trouble."

Finn returned with a cup of coffee for Sarah. She held the coffee below her lips with both hands and closed her eyes while taking in a deep breath, as if it comforted her. "I better just go lie down now. Excuse me." She stood and lumbered up the stairs, carefully balancing her coffee.

"I should analyze that data I captured with Josephine," Finn said. "I want to be prepared for her next appearance, if that's possible."

"And I should study the words in the book, I guess."

"The translation is next to it, on the desk. I wonder if a psychic has to say the words, because then you'll have to learn phonetically. I can help." He began moving away.

"We aren't there yet. We should find out more."

A thought occurred to Emmie, and from her pocket she dug out the key Betty had handed her before her death. She turned it over in her fingers before squeezing it, as if she might extract some powerful knowledge from that tiny object. "I'm thinking the same thing."

❧ 24 ❧

Sarah climbed into the guest-room bed, not bothering to climb under the furnished sheets. She lay on her side, staring at the gaudy wallpaper as the reddish-orange light from the setting sun streamed in through the unshaded window near her feet. Her stomach churned as if she'd eaten some spoiled food, and every muscle ached like she'd just finished working a twelve-hour shift at the hospital.

A weight pressed on her. Not necessarily physical—an emotional weight. Was it all part of the grief from her grandmother's passing? But seeing Betty die had rekindled those emotions, and the heaviness was even more unpleasant this time. Betty had looked about the same age as Sarah's grandmother. The same frail frame, focused eyes, and tenacious glow. Two powerful souls gone in a week.

The pain subsided as she closed her eyes and floated off, allowing the silence of the house to envelop her. Within moments, she was asleep.

She awoke to a whisper in her ear. A soothing voice of a woman she immediately recognized.

"Hey, Tiger."

Sarah opened her eyes, and she was back in her grandmother's house. The colorful bed quilt her grandmother had draped over her while tucking her in the night before still weighed her down. A porcelain ballerina doll sat on the nightstand next to the portrait of her mother's family. A sweet smell hung in the air —freshly baked cookies?—and a gentle breeze cooled the room through an open window.

Her grandmother's face peered down at her.

"Grandma?" Sarah smiled.

Her grandmother's grin stretched wide. "You overslept. Now let's get you up and ready to go on a walk with me. We love our walks together, don't we?"

Sarah nodded. "It's a lot of fun." She stared into her grandmother's warm eyes. They looked even more radiant than she'd ever seen.

A distant noise distracted her—somewhere at the back of her mind. She needed to remember something important, but that didn't matter now. It was her time to spend with her grandmother, and it was always fun. More fun than anything.

Sarah climbed out of bed and didn't bother to get dressed. She had slept in her clothes. "Shouldn't I change?"

"You look beautiful." Her grandmother caressed her face. "Don't let anyone tell you otherwise."

That was her grandmother. Always saying the sweetest things.

Sarah followed her to the door.

They paused behind the closed door, and her grandmother cracked it open, then turned back with a finger over her puckered lips "We need to keep quiet. Pepper's sleeping down the hall. Try not to disturb him."

Pepper was a friendly dog, a small black Terrier with thick fur, but full of energy, so it was better to let him sleep. He would plead with them to go with if they woke him up, and they needed an unencumbered escape from the house.

Sarah tiptoed down the hall beside her grandmother, with

the floors squeaking at every step. Pepper's hearing was incredible—he might come rushing out of his lair at any moment.

Sarah tried to move as stealthily as possible, following her grandmother's guidance. Going for a walk with her had been one of the joys in her life because of all the outrageously funny and fascinating conversations they'd shared. The subject didn't matter either—they could talk about *anything*—and if she was in a bad mood, then by the time she returned to the house she'd always felt like everything was okay.

Nausea swelled in Sarah's stomach as she proceeded along the hallway. She cringed and held her stomach. "Grandma."

The old woman stopped and glared back, now with furrowed brows. Again she held a finger in front of her lips. "Shh."

Sarah snapped her mouth shut, nodded, and forced a smile, holding back a groan as the pain in her stomach swelled. Not only was she ready to vomit, her head ached too, and every movement further down the hallway caused her to cringe. She clenched her hands into tight fists as she struggled to hold in the pain. It would be better outside. The sunlight blared in through an open window ahead. The air would be clean, she could clear her mind, and the pain would go away. Just a little further.

They headed down the stairs now. Pepper hadn't awakened, thank God, but she still tiptoed anyway, just a few paces behind her grandmother. Sarah didn't remember her parents dropping her off. Shouldn't she be at home now? Where was home? How had she gotten to her grandmother's house?

Her grandmother paused at the bottom of the stairs and smiled, breaking Sarah's train of thought. She waved Sarah down, trying to hurry her along because she had hesitated too long.

"Pick up the pace," her grandmother whispered.

Sarah caught up, and they almost danced toward the front door. Her grandmother's playful spirit was contagious. The sunlight coming in through the open windows around the living room and kitchen area brightened her mood. What would they talk about this time? It had been so long since they had last taken off walking in the countryside. How long had it been? Five, ten years? More than that? But her grandmother still looked the same now as she had back then.

Pushing aside the thought, Sarah continued.

Noises erupted from upstairs. Oh, no, they had awakened Pepper.

Her grandmother gestured toward the door, then opened it. "Hurry outside."

Sarah moved as quickly as she could.

"Get a move on it, Tiger. We've got a wonderful day ahead of us."

"Are we going to the park this time?"

"Yes, just a long, beautiful walk, and a little work. A pleasant day to share your thoughts. Aren't you going to bring along your book?"

Sarah stopped. "We're going for a walk, right Grandma?"

Her grandmother smiled. "Yes, but I know you like to read sometimes at the park. Bring it along, and we'll talk about your favorite books along the way."

Sarah spotted a novel across the room on the kitchen counter. She grabbed it and hurried back to her grandmother before heading out the door with her.

"*Sarah?*"

A woman's voice came from behind Sarah. It wasn't her mother's voice, but it was familiar. Someone who was trying to stop her from going for a walk? Instead of slowing down, Sarah sped up.

"Where are you going?" the woman asked.

Sarah rushed outside and paused in the front yard before her grandmother yanked her forward again.

"Hurry!" Her grandmother tickled her shoulder.

Sarah laughed and allowed herself to be led forward. The sun was so bright overhead and clear. The air soothed her nausea, just like her grandmother had suggested it would. She was right about so many things.

Someone pulled at Sarah's back and arm. Not her grandmother. Her mother again?

"What's wrong?" the woman asked.

"Go away," Sarah yelled. But the woman didn't let go.

Her grandmother continued pulling her as the woman now crossed between them, grabbing both her arms and holding her in place. Sarah thrashed to break free. "Leave me alone. I'm going for a walk."

"Are you sleepwalking?"

The question didn't make any sense. Sarah's eyes were wide open, and her grandmother scowled at her.

"Let me go."

The woman was holding her back from such a blissful day with the one person who had understood her better than anyone else. That was her mentor up ahead, waiting for her. It was her best friend, her hero. And this woman was ruining everything.

Sarah fought her, slamming her hands against the woman's body until Sarah stumbled and dropped back into the grass.

The world changed. The sunny day still surrounded her, but now her grandmother was gone and the woman who had stood in her way was Emmie.

"What's gotten into you? Should I get you to a doctor?"

Sarah scanned the lawn as reality struck her. She still longed for that stolen walk with her grandmother. Now the nausea returned, along with a pounding headache and a deeper emotional pain. None of it was real, but the experience reverberated through her as she calmed down on the grass. "I think I had a dream."

"I think you did too."

Sarah wiped the hair away from her face. "I dreamed about my grandmother. We were going for a walk and... you got in the way."

"Sorry." Emmie held out her hands and helped Sarah stand. She placed her palm against Sarah's forehead. "You don't have a fever. Let's get you back inside."

Sarah nodded and followed her toward the front door. "It was so real."

Emmie gestured to something in Sarah's hand. "Why did you bring that along?"

Sarah held up the French occult book. "Oh, God, I don't know."

❧ 2 5 ❧

E mmie opened the door to Sarah's room and peeked inside. Sarah was still lying in the same position as when Emmie had checked on her half an hour earlier. Sarah's purple hair was spilled out across the pillow, and her breathing was steady and calm. *Good. At least she is getting some proper sleep now.*

Sleepwalking wasn't something to be taken lightly, by all accounts. Luckily, Sarah hadn't gotten too far, and this was the first time Emmie had caught anyone in the act. But it was still unnerving to think what might have happened if she hadn't gotten distracted by a distant voice, an old woman's whisper, telling her to go outside. That soft voice had brought Sarah to mind, along with a small black dog, although there was no sign of any spirits nearby. With everything that had happened recently, they would need to keep an eye on her.

Sarah's chest rose and fell slowly, almost imperceptibly. Emmie closed the door as quietly as she could until the small click of the door latch broke the silence as she backed away.

Turning toward the hallway, she shuddered as Finn stepped up next to her. "Oh, you scared me."

"I scared *you?*" Finn gave a shadow of his usual smirk. "*I'm* the one that's scared, remember? How is she doing?"

"Still sleeping."

"She must be having a worse time than we thought."

Emmie nodded as they walked back down the hall toward Finn's room. The small pile of electronics on his bed showed where he'd been working with some of his equipment.

"She's definitely been through a lot," Emmie said. "I think that witnessing Betty's death also had a big impact on her. Not being able to save her must have been traumatic. All her skills as a nurse and the empath thing, and there wasn't anything she could do."

The floor of Finn's room was cluttered with cables and boxes of opened electronics, but on top of a wooden table in the center of the room he had laid out a laptop with cords snaking out of it in all directions.

"You really know what all those cords are connected to?" Emmie asked.

"I do."

"Do you ever take a break from that?"

"Not too often. It's quite interesting. I'm working on something now, just some of the strange interactions I mentioned earlier when dealing with Josie..."—Finn corrected himself—"*Josephine* this morning. The way she reacted when I focused the Beast device on her was unusual, like we said. I thought connecting both the devices not only physically, but through a separate piece of software on the Beast might push the boundaries a little and I'd see what happened."

"So what do you think happened?"

"I don't know yet. I haven't analyzed all the data. Unfortunately, it takes time to process everything and contemplate what I've captured. I'm combining technologies hoping to produce a different result than if I had used each of them separately. If I can push the EMF frequencies higher, or overlap them, then direct them out at the target, and combine those with the thermal camera, I can create a device that interacts with the paranormal rather than just receives data. I guess you could say it's my attempt to reach out and touch one of them."

"I thought you already did that with Josephine," she remarked wryly.

"Yeah, I sure did." He got a confused look on his face. "I can't get my head around it. It's just bizarre thinking that Josie wasn't... alive."

"I've never seen anything like her, either. I guess it's a learning experience for both of us."

Finn looked over at his devices. "I guess so. Lots to learn. I'll show you the results when I'm done."

"I'm sure you will, and I can't pretend I understood everything you said, anyway."

"Any sign of Josephine?" Finn asked. "I mean, I'm not seeking her out or anything."

"My guess is that something happened to her after Betty died. Maybe Betty succeeded in sending her somewhere, dragging her spirit away. I don't know."

"How would we know if she succeeded?"

"I don't know that either. I wish Betty were here to tell me."

Finn sat in front of his laptop and focused on the screen before typing for a few seconds. "At least things have quieted down since you arrived. Maybe the ghosts are afraid of you."

"I hope so. At least the bad ones like Josephine."

Emmie took a step toward the door. "I'm heading out for an evening walk."

The rich, dark orange sunlight streamed in through the open curtains. "Good idea, but I'd rather keep working on this. Go, get a little fresh air and your strength back. I can keep an eye on Sarah."

Emmie touched the phone in her pocket. And the key Betty had given her. *Use it*, the old woman had whispered. She didn't know why, but she preferred not to tell Finn what she was about to do. Not that he would stop her, but if he'd seen Betty give her the key, he'd be there already. But she needed quiet now, and a little time alone.

"Call me if you need anything." Emmie stepped into the hallway and looked back. "Don't let Sarah go out."

Finn nodded. "We'll be okay."

Outside the house, Emmie was glad to feel the fresh air again. The breeze was invigorating as she moved across the driveway toward the gravel road. She stared to her right, back down the road toward town, and spotted the clump of trees and roof of the house where Finn had told the police Betty had lived. Not too far to walk.

It seemed wrong to creep into Betty's house so soon after her death, even if she had given Emmie what appeared to be the house key. Could she have children who might show up? Or what if the police found her inside rummaging through Betty's things?

But Betty had explicitly told her to *use* the key. And had repeated to them over and over that there was no time to lose because Josephine was planning something awful.

How awful?

Maybe the key would answer that.

But Josephine alone could not free Victor, they'd discovered, so maybe they should visit the cemetery, and make sure the French damsel in distress hadn't seduced another poor sucker to do her bidding. If Josephine was still around, would she need to wait until it got dark? Or at least until the graveyard was empty?

Emmie had a few hours, she was sure. And maybe that would be enough. She walked out to the main road and headed right to Betty's house.

The boy she had seen earlier, David, was there, watching her approach. Maybe she would try to communicate with him again, but he was already backing away.

"Don't run!" Emmie waved and called out to him.

He darted off into the cornfield. No, that wasn't going to work. If she was going to take the time to listen to his story, she might need to sit out by the edge of the road and wait for *him* to approach. He would be like a wild animal learning to trust a stranger who offers it food.

With the gravel crunching beneath her shoes, Emmie walked the stretch of road down to Betty's house, passing the cornfield where the boy had disappeared.

Betty's place sat hidden behind several large oak trees in the front yard. It was an old single-story farmhouse without a farm. Just large enough for an unmarried librarian or a widow to spend her last years enjoying the solitude of country life. Not much landscaping around the yard, just a row of shrubs along one edge of the property, some potted flowers, and scattered roses in the front garden below the living room window. All the window shades were closed.

Emmie stepped up to the front and knocked, looking for signs of someone inside. No clues that the police had been there —not even a note warning anyone of Betty's death. Pressing her ear to the door, she listened for any footsteps or sounds of a pet inside. Nothing. She waited thirty seconds before placing the key in the lock. It didn't work.

She tried the door and found it unlocked. But was it burglary if she continued? Or breaking and entering? But she wasn't planning to steal anything or break anything. She imagined the ridiculous conversation she'd have with anyone who found her snooping around inside.

Never mind me. I'm just checking out this key Betty handed to me before she died. My name? Puddin' Tame.

She cracked the door open and peered in. All the lights were off and no sign of anyone inside. The shades over the other windows were closed too.

Emmie stared down at the key in her hand. *Well, she wanted me to have it, so it must open something.*

Glancing around, she took a deep breath and stepped inside.

🎋 26 🎋

Finn studied the shifting purple and blue blobs on the screen. Josephine's heat signature looked no more human than the slab of stone they'd buried her in, but there it was. A lifeless mass—moving and breathing—and it defied scientific explanation. Any other skeptic would view that and label it a fraud, but he'd seen it, held it, and... *kissed* it. He grimaced, especially when he thought that it had felt good.

He shuddered. Time to take a break from his work.

As he stretched his back, he looked around the room and again noticed all the furniture, but this time he remembered the caretaker's emphasis. It had all been there since the beginning.

Why hadn't he thought of that? His time at Caine House had already revealed some secrets, but there had to be more. What would he find hidden away? He could think of twenty places to look, or more. The basement, the pantry, the back porch, the storage area beneath the stairs, and a few smaller rooms on the main floor that he'd visited, but not *searched*. The previous tenants and the caretaker might have scrutinized it, but if all the furnishings were original, and there was so much of it, then *someone* must have left *something* behind.

They couldn't have removed *all* the secrets of Caine House.

All the ghosts, the thundering sounds of boots and men that he'd heard until Josephine's appearance—all the men who'd come to kill themselves here must have stashed away a clue as to the reason behind their deaths.

A bloody knife or a bag of bones?

A treasure?

Finn spoke into the still air as if Victor were listening. "What happened in this house, Vic? Certainly more than just spurn Josephine. Did she kill herself too? Did you do something terrible? Who locked you in your grave? You were a rich man, and I doubt you managed to sweep every dirty deed under the rug."

Under the rug.

Finn stared at the floor. A dark red mosaic rug took up most of the floor, with heavy furniture holding it in place. What would he find under there? A trap door? If he slid the dresser over, he could pull up a corner and take a peek. Was it worth the effort?

Why not?

It was an antique oak dresser, hand-crafted, and to lighten the work he removed all the drawers, inspecting them in the process for hidden compartments, and placed them on the bed.

Even without the drawers in place, the dresser was a monster to move. Easily over a hundred pounds. But he slid it far enough to free one side of the rug. Getting it back *on* the rug would be a challenge, but it didn't matter now. Pulling back the rug's corner by several feet, he revealed the wood floor beneath. No surprises, just several old coins, a lot of dirt, but nothing else. No trap doors or confession letters.

Leaving the dresser in place and empty for now, he eyed a small wood desk in the corner of the room. Maybe long ago they had used it to write letters. He had dismissed it earlier for practical reasons—not large enough to hold even his laptop—but it had a single drawer in the center and a mirror attached to the top. It looked more like a vanity table than anything he might use to write letters on.

Better check it out. He scrutinized the drawer and the backside, even reaching under it, running his fingers along the seams of the wood.

Again, nothing.

Okay, Finn, how far are you going to take this? Was he planning to search through the entire house? He grinned. He did have plenty of time.

Should he start upstairs? Sarah and Emmie now occupied the guest rooms, so maybe it was better to start on the main floor. Walking out of his room down the hallway, he passed their rooms. Their doors were closed. Sarah would be sleeping now, so he stepped cautiously along and down the stairs. He would feel awful if Sarah could not rest because of his quest.

Standing at the bottom of the stairs in the foyer, he scanned the area for a place to start. So many portraits of Victor stared back at him. He passed the smaller one with the eyes now carved out and stopped at the largest, main one hovering above him. Finn stared into Victor's eyes, transfixed at the realism of the painting. So lifelike.

"Who's haunting this house. You?"

Victor stared back.

Stepping past the portrait, a doorway across the room stood out. The door's frame lay flush with the wall, and he hadn't noticed it before. The caretaker hadn't taken him in there either. Probably a closet.

Finn walked over and tried the brass door handle. It opened to reveal a dark, stuffy room. He flipped on the light and stepped inside. The room was empty except for another door off in the corner, and more portraits lining the walls with another thick brown rug centered beneath the light. Nothing to clear away this time. He walked along, pulling up the edges of the rug as he circled it, but discovered only more dirt hiding beneath it.

The portraits on the walls of this room showed Victor and the five men, all in business suits, brandishing a rifle and a big grin. Victor's portrait was a little larger than the others' and sat alone on the far wall. Maybe they had used the room to hold meetings?

Finn strolled beside the walls and lifted each portrait just far enough to see behind it. Coming on another portrait of Victor, he pulled it back and spotted the outline of a small door.

"Bingo." His heart raced as he considered the possibilities. A safe?

Gently removing Victor's portrait and placing it on the floor, Finn pulled on the wooden doorknob. The door cracked open. Inside was a small shelf and a key similar to the one he'd found earlier that had opened the crypt.

Now to find what it belonged to. Taking the key, he scrutinized every part of the room, and his eyes stopped on the locked door he'd tried earlier. Would the shadow he'd encountered through the keyhole still be in there? Taking in a deep breath, he walked over to the door and tried the key in the door's lock. It snapped open.

"Now we're getting somewhere."

The room inside resembled an office with two old floor lamps flanking an antique secretary's desk that rose to the top of his head. Judging by its size, they had most likely assembled it in the room or built the room around it during its original construction. It was far too large to squeeze through the door.

It had at least twelve drawers in the main center area, all with brass handles and finely carved wooden doors. Victor must have dropped a fortune for that thing.

Finn didn't waste any time exploring it, going through every drawer and then pulling back the two main doors in the center that revealed even smaller compartments and a flat desk area.

"Drawers within drawers." He opened each of them, starting from the center and working his way across and then up, although he strained to get a look inside the ones along the top. Someone had stuffed a few of the drawers with stale yellow papers that revealed nothing of importance, and a smaller one contained several colorful suit buttons. He found a hand mirror with an ivory handle in another drawer and paused for a moment to look at himself. The reflection was slightly warped, but not bad for something crafted over a century earlier.

Pulling out and checking inside drawer after drawer, his hopes of finding anything of value or significance faded. Someone had most likely already scoured through them.

Still, he continued through to another compartment and found two small doors that wouldn't open. They were part of a larger piece, and after pulling out the main section a few inches, the two smaller doors opened and revealed four smaller wooden boxes behind them.

Finn rolled his eyes. "You're not making this easy for me, Victor."

But that's the point, isn't it?

He lifted out all four boxes and found them empty, but something didn't look quite right. The boxes didn't reach all the way to the back of the desk. Behind them, a solid wood wall stopped halfway.

Viewing the blocked opening from different angles, he spotted a hairline separating the wood running on the outside edge. He reached in and ran his fingers along it, pushing and pulling to confirm his suspicions. The wall moved. Wiggling it further, he slid it off to the side. A false wall. The hidden compartment opened, running to the back of the desk, but several papers and letters sat in the way.

He dug them out and looked them over. Business documents and personal letters from and to Victor Caine. One of the documents detailed the house's construction and the land surveys. Nothing of interest unless you were one of the town's hardcore historians.

Flipping through the opened letters, one of them was still sealed. Across the front it read:

"To whom it may concern, open upon my death. Victor Caine."

Finn didn't even debate whether or not to open it. "Try to stop me, Vic old boy!" he said defiantly, although he glanced around the room as if someone might catch him in the act while carefully tearing the letter open.

The handwriting was neat, but the English was difficult to decipher because of the cursive style. Still, Victor Caine had signed his name at the bottom. This should be interesting.

"There is a witch among you, but you need not fret, because I murdered her. Josephine Burdette was a lovely woman, and some will remember her as the beautiful French seductress who captured my heart as soon as she arrived in Lake Eden. Her skills in the dark arts amazed me the first day we met, but now she only wishes that my spirit suffers forever in purgatory.

Yes, I foolishly allowed the sweet Josephine to play with my heart for a time, but how could I have helped myself? Could you have danced with the devil better than I? So many men would have given up every worldly possession just to be held in her arms, but she chose my arms, and I fear I will lose far more than worldly possessions for my transgressions. But how do you subdue the power of a woman like that? She was untamable, and I had no choice but to act accordingly.

I write this as a warning to others. I loved her, but as my heart weakened my sensibilities and my decisions, her control over me became too great. Too much power and too many secrets dancing in her mind. A dagger to the throat was all it took, and it erased my problems in a single day.

I hope no one finds this letter because I believe I did a great service to this town by my actions. Lake Eden will always need me, and it should always revere my name.

But if the witch Josephine ever rises from her grave, then someone must put her down again. Below, you will find detailed notes on the ceremony I performed to achieve that. Her heart is black, and she would stop at nothing to achieve her revenge on me and the town."

"A little too late, Victor," Finn mumbled.

The whole story behind the letter was something that Betty might have clarified, but it was clear enough why Josie had hated Victor so much. No one hates that much without having loved as much first.

The man had been a cold bastard, that was for sure.

He gathered the documents and letters, setting them aside. This was something he definitely needed to tell Sarah and Emmie immediately. It might help them learn how to imprison Josephine again if she returned.

Finding no more letters or documents in the desk, he closed it up again and left the room in the same condition he had found it, minus a few documents nobody would ever miss.

Silence flooded the house. He went upstairs to check on Sarah. No need to wake her up with his find, but he was anxious to tell *someone* about it. Stopping in front of her door, he listened for any sounds of her inside. Nothing. He would need to keep the news to himself a little longer.

Still, maybe she was sitting up in bed or busy doing something else.

He tapped lightly on the door. "Sarah?"

No answer.

He put his hand on the door handle and turned it slowly while pushing at the same time. The wood door scraped against the doorframe, but opened just far enough for him to see that Sarah's bed was empty.

Oh good, she's awake.

"Sarah?" he called a little louder.

He opened the door further, catching sight of the cup of coffee he'd given her earlier. It was still full. She hadn't even taken a sip! *Nobody likes my coffee.*

He stepped inside, peering around the door.

She was gone.

Gone? Gone where? How could he have missed her footsteps coming down those squeaky stairs? But that back office was quiet, built for solitude.

Stepping out into the hallway, he called, "Sarah? Are you here?"

Not upstairs, at least. Finn rushed downstairs. She was an adult, and could take care of herself under normal circumstances, but nothing was normal lately. He circled past the kitchen on the way to the front door. The French occult book was missing from the counter.

Why would Sarah take that?

Arriving at the front door, he stared outside. Emmie's car was still in the driveway, and they had arrived together.

Out for a walk?

His heart beat faster as his mind jumped back to her room and the sight of the coffee sitting there, untouched. She had loved the smell, carried it upstairs with her and then not touched it.

Just like Josie.

27

A strange odor caught Emmie's nose as she stepped into Betty's house, not unlike a scented candle or if someone had burned an incense stick recently. The smell was familiar, a woody and smoky fragrance that reminded her of...

Mom and Dad. They had filled their offices with similar scents; these were amulets, they had said. Scents inside sachets and tiny wooden boxes that could ward off or reveal spirits. Betty had smelled like that behind Caine House.

But the odd, elusive memories of her parents did nothing to lessen the awkward feelings at entering a stranger's home. A dead stranger's home.

No sounds, except the refrigerator's hum in the kitchen nearby.

She stepped further into the dining area, and the linoleum floor cracked beneath her feet. The dishwasher sat open, half empty, with two cupboards open above it as if Betty had left it in a hurry. No family pictures on the refrigerator or on the walls. She had set the kitchen table with four plates as if she had been expecting guests. Had she planned to invite her new neighbors over for a meal and then abandoned the idea after sensing something was off? She must have *known*.

Moving into the living room, Emmie spotted bookcases crammed with paperbacks and hardcovers. A few scattered boxes around the room and only one photo, that of a younger Betty standing next to an older man. Maybe her father?

Nothing out of the ordinary about Betty's house, so why had she given Emmie the key? Maybe the key wasn't intended for something inside the house?

Down the hallway, she peered into what was obviously an office. No sign of a computer, but several open books stacked on top of each other surrounded by scattered papers showed where the old woman had worked. Emmie flipped on the overhead light and read some of the titles on her desk: *Psychic Believer, Secret History of Occult Magic, Days of the Initiated, Dictionary of Occult Spells, Book of Witchcraft, Native American Spirits*. Some of them she remembered seeing in her parents' own study back in the house long ago. None appeared to be special or antique, like the French book.

A long line of photo albums filled one area of a bookcase. Emmie removed one and flipped through the pages. There were several photos of Betty next to different strangers.

She stopped at one photo a few pages into the book. It showed Betty by Emmie's parents and... Emmie—her preteen self. She couldn't have been over eight or nine in that photo, but she didn't remember the moment at all. Her heart sank as she stared into the beaming faces of her parents. Her mother's arm was around Emmie's shoulder, pulling her in.

Protecting me.

Had her parents only forced her through years of meditating and communicating to prepare her for more dangerous years ahead?

Could Betty have been right in saying they hadn't pushed her enough? *The ghosts will always find you.*

That thought was like destiny, and Emmie pushed it away. She continued searching through the photo books, but all the other names and faces were unfamiliar. If Betty had intended for her to find something important, then this was not the place.

There were only two bedrooms in the house, and within a few minutes Emmie had circled through them without finding anything unusual. She headed out toward the kitchen again and noticed an open doorway in the corner. Walking over and glancing down into the darkness of the basement, she flipped on the light and without hesitating started going down the steps. The basement's stale air flooded around her. There had to be some relevant information within all the clutter.

Black paneling covered the walls of the basement, and two small barred windows up near the ceiling were painted black, effectively blocking out any sunlight. A little unusual, considering that the area was empty.

On the other side of the basement, however, was a single doorway painted black along with everything else. Above the frame of the door on a small wooden shelf, stood several statues of creatures and skulls. Some of them reminded Emmie of gargoyles. Put there to keep the spirits from entering?

Emmie headed for the door and spotted a padlock on the door handle.

That's where the key goes. Emmie had no doubt it would work. She pulled it out and fit it into the lock. *This is it.* The padlock snapped open, and she left it hanging in place as she opened the door slowly as if someone—or some *thing*—inside might try to get out if she wasn't careful.

She flipped on the light and was confronted with symbols and candles and books and pentagrams hanging from the ceiling. This is where Betty had wanted her to go. The room was an office like the one upstairs, but this one contained her hidden life: all the books and occult artifacts Emmie's parents had owned during her childhood, and then some.

A desk sat in the corner with a single chair in front of it. She pulled it back and sat down, making herself comfortable while scanning the books and occult literature.

Many of the artifacts were archaic, as if Betty had been working to build her own personal museum. Some were exotic, resembling Egyptian items straight from the pyramids; others were disfigured stone statues an ancient Asian dynasty might have used as amulets or for atonement; there was a small, hand-made child's doll—vaguely resembling a human—made from animal bones and torn strips of cloth that reminded Emmie of voodoo. If truly old, the objects might have been worth a lot of money, but she doubted Betty had locked the room for the monetary worth of its contents. Here, Betty had gathered treasures of dark knowledge that only someone with deep insights could decipher.

Emmie scanned over the titles along the edge of the desk and stopped on two thick leather-bound books. It wasn't the books she was interested in, but instead a yellowing envelope poking out between them. She pulled it out, opened it, and skimmed over the handwritten pages. The first words grabbed her attention.

"My Revered Master,

My esteemed Master Guides,

My friends and fellow Skilled Perceptives,

As is the custom and our duty when spirits of great power and evil abide still among us, incapable or unwilling to pass on, I hereby write the account of my dealings in the town of Lake Eden, Minnesota.

As you know, our sister Josephine Burdette left New Orleans to help in the case of hauntings in this newly formed town on the 20th of April 1902. She was contacted by a letter from the mayor of Lake Eden, Victor Edward Caine, who wanted to rid the place of ghosts and malicious apparitions.

You know that I bore Josephine a great affection. We shared a home in New Orleans and were close confidantes. It is not, therefore, to be wondered at that she should write to me from Lake Eden to tell me about the apparitions.

I only later learned that she neither informed the council of the trip nor wrote to you from the site as all of us are meant to do.

The reasons for her secrecy, I'm afraid, became clear in letters that she kept sending me.

The man, Victor Caine, she described as handsome, strong and compelling. His house was haunted, and she learned the spirits were his business associates. These men had trooped, one by one, to Caine House, the mansion the mayor had built for himself, and either shot or hung themselves on his property.

She was at first puzzled by these coincidences, and I assumed from her early letters that these were the spirits she was meant to purge. As we know, it is difficult to do so without understanding the spirits' reason for dwelling in our plane, but suicides rarely know they are dead.

I encouraged her, therefore, to discover the reason for their dwelling —what trouble, grief or guilt did they have, which drove them to self-harm?

To my surprise, her next letters were of a more confidential nature, and this I did not discuss with anyone. As my friend, she confessed to the development of a wild passion for Victor Caine. In her estimation, no man could compare, or had such strength and purpose. His plans for the city, his vision, his energy—and, I suspect, something more sensual—had her besotted.

She described him as being equally besotted by her.

We are not, in our midst, prone to making moral judgments about love or passion, but I cautioned my friend that until she understood those spirits lingering there and purged them, she ought not to fall into a hopeless passion for the man who was being haunted.

My advice fell on deaf ears. All her letters were full of Victor Caine. She didn't expect to return to New Orleans, but hoped, in the near future, that I should be able to visit her when she became lady of the house and of the city.

Concern for my friend again made me importune her about the spirits. At first, she said the situation was "resolved" without giving more details.

Then a letter of a different sort arrived. Passion remained, but suspicion had made its appearance. Caine was changing, she said. He spoke of political alliances and might be courting a young heiress in Saint Paul. She spoke of treachery that he would pay for if he tried to throw her aside like a worn rag.

This language was not what I knew and expected from her, but letters began to arrive almost frantically, and her tone got ever darker.

Finally, she spoke of danger, and said she must tell me that Caine had not contracted her to be rid of the spirits of his business associates, but of other spirits who had driven his men to suicide."

Emmie's eyes widened as she read, and her heart accelerated a little. Her gaze was stuck on that sentence as if it refused to move down and read something even more terrible.

"Mr. Caine had summoned my sister to lock the souls of fifty-seven inno-cents, as she herself described them, below ground.

These men, women and children were the original settlers of the fertile land around Lake Eden, a land which Victor Caine and his associates craved to found a town..."

A heaviness swept through Emmie's chest, and she looked away for a moment. *How could this be true?* Her pulse beat in her throat like a tiny hammer.

"They would not move anywhere else, and Caine and his men would not choose a different land when this location had ore, stone, a rich soil, and all he needed.

So, they killed the settlers. They shot them all. Even women. Even children and babes."

The letter hung from Emmie's hand as she fell against the back of the chair. Tears had blurred her vision now, and a boy leaped into her imagination—David. Running through corn-fields, looking behind him in terror, the back of his shirt drenched with blood from the merciless bullets of Caine or his men.

The settlers had been martyrs, but not to the Native Americans. Instead, to greed. To ambition.

She contemplated the revelation for several minutes before composing herself enough to continue reading.

"Mr. Caine and his accomplices furthermore placed the blame on the Sioux tribe and obtained help from the local government to massacre them too.

But it wasn't the Sioux who stayed behind to haunt him. Perhaps some of their tribe helped them to pass on or quieted their spirits, but no one had done that for the innocent settlers. They wandered in grief, looking for their children or their parents, appearing to Caine's men, who had killed them, until even those calloused hearts were driven to suicide, all of them first making a pilgrimage to their leader, Victor Caine, as if to ask for guidance, help—or blame him too?

Only Caine himself remained impervious to the tragedy he had perpetrated, and even to the death of his former friends. It was not the spirits of his men that bothered Caine, Josephine said. They could stay around—she thought that, in a way, they even made him feel less isolated.

It was the settlers she had to silence, and already lost in a passion for the man and believing his lies, she had locked their souls where they were buried, in a mass grave.

A mass grave over which Caine, hoping to seal them further, built a monument.

Her last letters spoke of Caine changing further, showing ever less fervor for her. Of a calculating glint appearing in his eyes and a hardening determination in his face when she reminded him they were in this together, or till death parted them.

Her letters stopped.

Although her soul already seemed lost, this is when I obtained your approval to come to Lake Eden and discover more about the spirits here and what had happened to our Josephine.

In town, I did not even have to ask. Gossip made sure I learned quite quickly that the Frenchwoman who acted as housekeeper to the mayor and founder had left, and that Mr. Caine was looking for a replacement.

I applied and obtained the position; it was not difficult, given the shortage of skilled labor.

My own plainness, I supposed, served me better than Josephine's beauty, as Mr. Caine never approached me unduly. He rather liked to keep his distance. The maids did speak of noises and groaning in the house, and more than one left during my time there.

I knew what these were due to. I could see the spirits, but none were Josephine.

Yet a dark energy centered in a stone structure at the back. Only Mr. Caine had the key, and I had to wait to get it. And my suspicions were then confirmed.

It was the grave of Josephine. I do not know how he managed to lock her in, although we have studied that when a soul is weak before another, even a person without gifts can subdue it by following the rites. And she was weak when it came to him.

But by now such dark energy resided around her grave, pulling at me, and I never could enter the structure again. She remained there, churning in rage and unable to escape.

Mr. Caine never showed the slightest remorse for anything he had done, though I often heard him muttering to himself in the house. Could he converse with ghosts? I believe he only ever wanted to talk to himself and constantly emphasize how right he had been to kill so many people. How weak, perhaps, his co-conspirators had been. How little he feared temptresses such as Josephine, or anyone dead or alive.

The worst part is that the town celebrated him. "I had a vision and I achieved it," he would say. Everyone agreed.

And it was the most prosaic of things that got him in the end. Only a few months after I arrived, and before he could culminate his achievements by marrying the heiress, he contracted dysentery and fell severely ill.

A man of his constitution might have survived, but ironically his own friends didn't allow it. I saw their spirits crowding around him as if to help him, but in fact feeding off his energy and suffocating him with their mistaken solicitousness.

He died enfeebled and confused enough for me to imprison his spirit with the cross and the words of death. Just as he had done to Josephine.

Just as Josephine had done to the innocent.

These two spirits stay locked in Lake Eden. And the innocent, I'm afraid, must stay locked too, for their poor trampled souls might seek vengeance upon their release, and somehow convince someone to free their murderer, which would result in ruin for many.

The imprisonment of these innocents saddens me, but Caine and Josephine are not the worst spirits we have encountered. We are too few fighting this great battle against Devils and Demons, and only a mystic of great strength can force two such recalcitrant and vengeful souls to pass.

For the moment they are locked, but they must one day be sent to their final rest, which, I'm afraid for my erstwhile friend, will be in hell.

I urge the council, however, to think of the fifty-seven souls unfairly imprisoned, doomed to confusion and to relive their torment eternally. I urge you to send here, as soon as possible, a Master Perceptive capable of dispatching the evil spirits of Victor Caine and Josephine Burdette and free the innocent souls to their eternal rest."

The letter ended and tears flowed down Emmie's cheeks as she folded it again and placed it back where she'd found it. This was at least some of the information Betty had meant to disclose to them, although the old woman hadn't gotten the chance. Emmie was meant to find it all, and, no doubt, many more revelations were within her reach.

She spotted an old, faded black-and-white photo on the wall of a woman in a white dress and small, decorative hat, the kind of photo they used to make in the old West where nobody smiled. Inspecting the photo more closely, she saw the same necklace Josephine had worn during her appearance in the crypt. Now the face was clear—it *was* Josephine. Her cold stare sent a chill through Emmie. That same woman had almost killed her.

Another row of books sat beside her. Thinner than all the others, but there were dozens of them, each labeled by year going all the way back to 1922. Emmie spotted the year her parents died and pulled it out.

Opening the book to the first page, she gasped at its contents. A page of notes written by Betty regarding voicemail messages Emmie's parents had left on Betty's phone. They had found Victor's cross for sale in the back of a Minneapolis occult bookstore, and had plucked it up before it fell into the wrong hands or another collector could conceal it from the world. The discovery alarmed them, and they pleaded for help in putting it back where it belonged. They noted the recent strange phenomena surrounding Lake Eden, and had connected it to Victor's missing cross.

Below the notes, Betty wrote that she had received the voicemails too late, having inadvertently allowed her phone's battery to die and hadn't noticed the issue until the next day. Her parents had already acted on the discovery by then, probably thinking she had ignored them or didn't understand the significance of their find.

"A terrible tragedy occurred with the death of Ed and Shannon Fisher. Of course, I would have stopped at nothing to return it had I only received their letter sooner. It pains me greatly that I couldn't have been there with them to put Victor back in his place."

The next few pages contained several newspaper articles detailing various unexplained outbreaks in the town. A swarm of locusts had devastated local crops, and many residents exhibited radiation-like illnesses, such as frequent vomiting and blistering skin burns, even for those who rarely went outdoors. And more events, like miles of land littered with thousands of dead crows. So many dead birds around the lake that boaters spent days scooping their rotting carcasses from the shoreline to stop the incessant stench and prevent the spread of whatever had killed them. Another article talked about the alarming surge of miscarriages, with the birth rate dropping to near zero in the following months.

The locals had blamed the mysterious events on pollution or poison in the water, maybe erupting from a geologic disturbance deep below the lake. Those were the theories discussed in the articles, but none of them listed any scientific evidence or connections between the events. A few surrounding churches declared the bizarre events as a sign of the coming apocalypse.

Had Victor's release caused all of that? The thought terrified her.

But how could the locals have known the true reason for their troubles? Even if they had heard about Victor's evil deeds and his grave, they wouldn't have understood or believed it. Only someone with a special kind of perception... a Master Perceptive... could have known what to do.

So it made sense that her parents had purchased the cross and had tried to put it back, since they couldn't find anyone powerful enough like Betty to help them. They must have felt that they had no choice, understanding the significance of its removal, and had rushed it back to Victor's grave to prevent more destruction.

On the next page, Betty noted again how much she grieved for Emmie's parents after perishing in the struggle to return the cross. She had put Victor back in his grave and soon after, the inexplicable events surrounding Lake Eden had stopped. Within days, all was quiet again.

"If they only knew of the sacrifice made to return the cross and how close they had come to total destruction! I will need to stay nearby to watch over both Victor's and Josephine's graves for fear that another poor soul might recklessly release him again. I only pray these old bones survive long enough to pass along this noble duty to one more physically capable."

She described purchasing the "adequate" house down the road from Caine House and vowed to check on Victor's and Josephine's grave regularly. Renting Caine House wasn't an option, given the strained funds for the council, and for herself, but she had a view of the Caine House driveway from her upstairs office window, and could monitor everyone who entered and left.

"If Josephine ever gets out and is allowed to pursue her vengeance against Victor, then all hell would break loose. Combined, their conflict could destroy more than just Lake Eden."

A footstep scraped against the floor of the basement outside the room. She turned to face Sarah, who was standing in the doorway wielding a knife and grinning with wide eyes.

28

Sarah was nauseous, but she couldn't stop moving forward. Her head ached as she trudged along the gravel road toward Betty's house. The evening weather was something straight out of a fairytale, with partly cloudy skies and a gentle breeze blowing through her hair. The grass and corn in the nearby fields sizzled as their leaves rustled in the wind. Not too hot, not too cold. Just right.

Reminds me of an evening in the countryside near Paris.

Sarah caught herself. Paris? Paris, France? Why would I think such a thing? And where am I going? I should be back at the house lying down right now. My body doesn't feel right. I should be sleeping.

No time to sleep, girl, you've got things to do. Shh, don't get in the way. I'll take care of everything.

Take care of what? I think I'm going to throw up.

It won't take long. Just a short walk, so don't resist or things will get even more painful for you.

Sarah slowed and tried to stop walking, but something pushed her forward. Her leg muscles operated as if on autopilot. She continued with her chin up, and a grin stretched across her face.

And she held the French occult book in her hand. *Why?* She couldn't read French anyway, but she couldn't let go of it. Now it seemed more important than ever.

Was she sleepwalking again? That had to be it. But she was aware of everything this time, and there was no one to interfere with wherever her subconscious directed her.

She strained to break herself out of the sleep, shaking her head two times and pinching her arm, but she continued without a pause. If she screamed, would Emmie or Finn hear her? She tried.

A moan escaped through her tightened lips. Please, break me out of this horrible dream.

Don't bother fighting it, ma petite, *or I will have to squeeze that little neck of yours. You shouldn't have interfered. You're lucky I don't throw you over a cliff right now.*

Sarah's eyes widened and her heart beat faster. Those were not her thoughts. What was happening? She hurried along the edge of the road toward Betty's house. She needed to find Emmie as soon as possible. Something was very wrong.

Mixed in with her own nausea and pain, a deep hatred flowed through her, and she visualized the face of Victor Caine. She would see him suffer for all eternity as soon as *the girls* were under control. Those who had betrayed her would die a thousand deaths.

Sarah hovered on the edge of vomiting, but the voice inside prevented her from making it happen.

Josephine?

Bull's-eye, girl. Stop struggling so much. You're a weak vessel, and this won't take long. If you stop fighting me, I may let you live. No sense in destroying a petite fille *like yourself with so much promise. Why destroy your sweet face over a little inconvenience like me? I only want what I want. I will finish Victor, and then I will move along and rest in peace like a good little spirit. Trust me, I'm doing the world a favor.*

Why do you hate Victor so much? What did he do to you?

I've been asleep for over a hundred years, chained to that grave after he betrayed me. I will get revenge. I won't stop until I do.

What do you intend to do?

Watch me.

Betty's house was not far ahead, maybe a couple of hundred feet from the front door. The windows were dark, with no sign of anyone inside.

Sarah struggled to push Josephine's spirit away from her. She clenched her fists and her chest shuddered as she attempted to regain control of even one part of her body long enough to stop Josephine's advance. The added pressure tensed her mind and body even further before she gave in.

Stop your resistance, or you will get the same punishment as Betty.

Why are we going to Betty's house?

You'll find out soon enough.

A car approached from the distance, coughing up a cloud of dust behind it. If she could collapse onto the gravel road, maybe the driver would see her fall and call an ambulance. Maybe that would delay Josephine's plans long enough to get Emmie's help.

But forcing herself to collapse proved impossible. Not only did she continue on her way, but she also smiled and waved to the driver. It was an older man behind the wheel, and he waved back, passing her in a white truck. Her first opportunity had failed.

Sarah crossed Betty's lawn and circled around the house to the back door. Without thinking about it, Sarah knew Emmie was inside the house, and Josephine planned to kill her.

If I can just warn her somehow. Sarah's mouth clamped shut as she entered through the unlocked door and crept inside. No way to open her mouth to scream. Each breath heaved in and out through her nose.

You can't hurt her. She didn't do anything to you.

You have proved yourselves to be troublesome. If you warn her, I will kill you both.

Sarah moved toward the basement door, inching forward like

a prowler while random noises coming from the basement caught her ear.

Emmie, run.

She can't hear you; lucky for you.

Josephine, don't hurt her.

Sarah was forced to detour to the kitchen, where she scooped up a long butcher's knife from the counter. She checked the blade, staring at her own frightened face in the reflection.

Stepping down the basement stairs slowly, methodically, Sarah strained with all her strength to lose her balance. If she could trip and fall forward, it would warn her friend of the approaching danger, but her body didn't listen—she plodded powerlessly along.

As her feet touched the cement floor of the basement, she spotted Emmie with her back turned toward her in a room at the far side. Sarah approached without blinking, ready to charge forward with the knife if her surprise attack failed. She held up the knife, ready to pounce.

Emmie, run! Sarah screamed inside, but not even a gasp escaped her throat. She crept up to the room's open door, now only inches away, while Emmie focused on a book held up near her chest.

Sarah pushed against Josephine's spirit with every bit of strength left in her. Josephine's grip on the knife loosened just a little, but it was enough.

The knife dropped, clanking against the concrete floor, and Emmie spun around with a startled expression.

Sarah slammed the door shut before slipping the padlock on the latch and clicking it locked. At least Emmie was alive.

Josephine's frustration surged. She flipped off the light switch next to the door and backed away. *It won't make a difference, ma petite. We'll come back for her later.*

"Sarah," Emmie yelled from inside the sealed room. "What are you doing? Open the door!"

Sarah laughed, even without wanting to, and turned back up

the stairs. Emmie screamed and yelled for help until the sound of her voice disappeared outside.

A tear ran down Sarah's cheek as she walked back to the road and headed toward town.

Here I come, Victor.

29

E mmie ran to the door, with the only light coming in through a narrow slit in the center. She slid the small metal door at the top open and stared through it, watching as Sarah stepped up the stairs without looking back.

"Sarah, let me out." Emmie pounded her fists on the door. "You can't leave me down here. Are you sleepwalking again? What are you thinking?"

Sarah just laughed.

But the truth was obvious. Sarah wasn't even herself. Her grandmother's death and then Betty's had affected her deeply, and she had become open to the psychic invasion of someone like Josephine. The circumstances had given Josephine a perfect opportunity to manipulate another victim, and that was where she had disappeared—into Sarah.

The darkness plunged in around Emmie as she continued to pound the door for a few more seconds before giving up. Nobody else would hear her anyway. Caine House was too far away for her shouting to make any difference, and her hands already hurt. Now she wished the police would come, even if it became embarrassing. She needed to stop Josephine and get Sarah back.

Straining her eyes to see anything in the room under the trickle of light, she scavenged through the items around the desk. She pushed aside books and papers, accidentally knocking an object from the wall in the process. It crashed to the floor. Something made of wood, by the sound of it.

There's got to be something in here I can use to get out. Betty wouldn't have allowed the room to become a jail.

Emmie dug through each drawer and door within the desk but found nothing that might help her escape or even light the way. As she turned back toward the door, something tickled her nose. She swatted it away. A spider?

I can handle a spider.

She pressed her hands against her pockets. Why hadn't she brought along her cellphone? She always had it with her, but she remembered she'd left it on Finn's kitchen counter.

Emmie's heart sank as she contemplated what might happen to Sarah if she didn't get out of there soon. And how long would it take Finn to come looking for them? Within the faint light, she ran her fingers along the edge of the door. Maybe there was a way to pull the door pins out? Or smash through it with a heavy object? Nothing like that in the room. The chair at the desk was just a rickety wooden thing, not heavy enough to make a difference. She glanced up at the ceiling. Could she break through the floorboards? The house *was* old. Maybe some of the boards were rotting, and even if she could pull one of them down, she could squeeze through.

She stared at the door. Or there could be a psychic solution. If she could focus really hard on the lock, maybe she could move it. She had never tried anything like that before, so why not?

After focusing for a few seconds, she gave up. Ridiculous. She was a psychic, not telekinetic. With all the spirits out there in the world waiting for her help, now she couldn't even help herself. Who would come to her rescue?

Nobody around, except...

One spirit came to mind. Someone nearby, and she even knew his name. David. Would he come if she called him?

It was worth a try. Emmie closed her eyes and focused on the boy's face as well as she remembered it. David. She pictured his clothes and bare feet, and the bloody hole in his back. She opened herself to communicate with him.

David, please come down here and unlock the door, if you can. Maybe it wouldn't do any good, anyway. David might not understand how to help her if he showed up, and there was no guarantee he could physically interact with anything like the Hanging Girl had done. Betty had said the Hanging Girl had grown solid from Emmie's and Sarah's combined powers, so perhaps the same could happen with David, as they had seen him together.

All he has to do is remove the padlock from the door.

She focused more intently, now imploring David to get there quickly. She took a deep breath. Plenty of air, but she already felt claustrophobic, and she might be stuck in that room for hours before Finn would think to search for her. She tried not to think about it and pushed away her anxiety.

Meditate and communicate.

David's image hovered on the edge of her thoughts, and she strained to see him clearly like her parents had taught her so long ago.

If I get out of here, I'm going to practice until it hurts. I'll meditate and communicate until I can call up the devil himself.

Well, no, maybe not that far.

Within a minute, gentle footsteps squeaked down the wooden stairs of Betty's basement. Peering out through the small opening in the door, she saw David—and he appeared solid now, stepping on the basement floor. He moved toward the locked door, his bare feet slapping against the cement.

Emmie gestured toward the lock with her eyes. "David. Please unlock the door. I've got the key here with me. I'll give it to you." She pulled it from her pocket and poked it out through the opening as far as she could. "Just take the key, unlock the padlock, then lift it off the latch. Can you do that?"

David stopped and stared at the key with a fearful expression.

"Remember me? I'm Emmie. I saw you outside."

David shook his head, then lifted a hand to his chest as if in great pain. He winced and took a step back. "They shot me."

"I know, David. I know who they were. Bad men. Just six bad men. Don't be scared. I can help you, but you need to open this door for me. Take the key from me and remove the lock. Okay?"

The boy looked suspiciously into Emmie's eyes, then at the key again. His eyes teared up. "They shot my Ma and Pa too. Why did they shoot us?"

"They were bad. I promise I'll help you find out if you unlock the door."

David stepped to the door now, keeping his eyes fixed on Emmie. He reached toward the key, but his fingers passed through it. He formed a confused expression. "I can't grab it."

"You can, David, if you just focus on it. Just try really hard. I know you can."

He tried again, now wincing, and finally plucked it from her fingers. Their skin touched for a moment—his was like ice—before he stepped back again. His gaze dropped to the door's lock, but she couldn't see if he'd grabbed it or not.

Emmie nodded. "Just use the key to open it, then lift it off. You can do it."

Something rattled against the other side of the door. Metal scraped against metal until something clinked against the basement floor.

The door loosened, and she pushed it open. It passed through David's spirit as it swung out.

Emmie felt the urge to hug him for rescuing her but held back. A sudden outburst might frighten him away. She left the room and turned back to him. "Thank you, David. Do you live in the cornfield?"

He looked around with a confused expression. "I don't remember. I want to go home."

"I'll help you get back home, I promise. Thank you for getting me out of there. I'll do the same for you, right after I find my friend Sarah. She's lost too, and something awful will happen to her if I don't get to her soon." Emmie moved halfway up the stairs, then paused and turned back. "I won't forget you, David."

She hurried upstairs, and David followed her all the way outside, stopping near the edge of the road as she continued toward Caine House. She glanced back a minute later, but he was gone.

Gasping in the clean evening air, she kept an eye out for any sign of Sarah. Had she gone back to hurt Finn?

And how would they stop great evil spirits at war with each other and capable of harming so many?

As she rushed up the drive, she met Finn, who was running out, his eyes bulging. What had happened now?

"Sarah!" he cried out.

"Yes, she—"

"She's freaking Josephine!"

30

Josephine walked along the gravel road toward the cemetery. All the things that had given her pleasure while alive, like the brilliant orange sunset and the clean air, meant nothing anymore. There was only the hatred burning inside, and the resolve to get to Victor's grave as soon as possible.

She had gotten hold of a body that could remove that cross. *Cette merde de croix!* She didn't need to seduce or cajole any men to do her bidding—*she* was going to do it. And in the body of another woman, too.

It was fun moving Sarah along, and controlling her like a puppet was easy. The gift to control others was difficult to master and often difficult to hold for a long time, but this girl's defenses were weak. Empaths put themselves out there for everyone, and she had exhausted herself trying to keep that ugly old woman from dying, which had been the perfect opening for an invasion.

Josephine waved at yet another passing car, just for the fun of it. A young girl in the passenger seat reciprocated the wave. How would the girl respond if she knew she were waving at a ghost? Josephine chuckled to herself.

Victor's image flashed through her mind again. Always at the center of her perception, the memories of what he had done to her burned and stung. She had opened herself to him, given herself up to him, believed him even when she knew he was lying, and that was the only reason he'd managed to lock her up with a cross and a few words.

She would make sure Victor suffered a thousand, a *million* deaths, and soon. Releasing Victor would be a simple matter now, and she imagined his expression when he rose from the grave, assuming that he was free. Ghosts didn't know the difference between life and death, or only some knew it. Joy would fill his face, but she would grab his spirit by the throat and drag him into the thrashing teeth of his victims.

Then she would take Sarah's body back to the house and burn it down. She would leave nothing of the man who had dared to destroy her. His soul would linger in perpetual terror for all eternity. She longed to hear Victor screaming. Oh, she would sing like a sweet bird as Victor's demons carried out their sweet justice on his snared soul.

Prends garde à toi... she sang now. *Prends garde à toi.*

She slowly moved along the gravel road, not feeling the weight of the human form she had stolen. She existed within the girl's body, carried along like a princess riding on the arms of servants.

Do you feel my anger? Josephine pushed the thought into the girl's mind.

Sarah grumbled, but didn't speak.

It's wise for you to keep your silence. I can hurt you. Your desperation to escape annoys me, but that will be your burden to bear until I make things right for my soul. I will get my revenge.

"Why did Victor betray you?"

What game are you playing with me now, girl? Do you think you can trick me? Lower my defenses or distract me?

"No trick. I can help you move on, allow your spirit—"

And let him get away with it? Josephine yelled within the girl's mind, making her voice crack like a whip until she winced.

"Others might suffer..."

Then let them suffer. I'll tell you why Victor betrayed my trust. Men are evil, and above all, they are selfish. If you survive the day, you would be wise to be careful. The best piece of advice I can give you is this: Don't trust them. They will always betray you in the end.

"How did he betray you?"

Victor's face played like a movie in Josephine's mind, his laughter and promises. *Have you been in love, girl?*

"I don't know."

If you don't know, it hasn't happened. You'd know if you were willing to do anything for someone. Any crime, any deed.

"What did he do?"

Be quiet, girl. He will pay, so it doesn't matter.

"You could have resisted him."

Josephine laughed. *You don't know anything. You're like a silly baby. No one knows how to love anymore. Or hate. It should take everything you have.*

"I don't want that. I want peace."

Peace comes in your grave, if you are lucky. I can put you there.

"Who put Victor in his grave? Shouldn't you deal with them first?"

Only someone like me could have put him there. I don't care who it was. I'm dead, girl, and unlike him, I know it. So I have nothing to lose.

"You're no better than Victor."

Josephine snapped the girl's mouth shut. *I'm done with you.*

The edge of the cemetery came into view.

❦ 31 ❦

Emmie and Finn scanned the roads, fields, and even the ditches around Caine House for any sign of Sarah, then hurried back toward Emmie's car. The evening sky grew darker as thick clouds rolled in.

How long would Josephine manipulate Sarah, and what would she do once her friend no longer served a purpose? Emmie cringed. With any luck, Sarah had broken away from the spirit's grasp and was wandering, dazed and confused, and they would find her.

Finn shook his head. "I'm sure she took Sarah to remove Victor's cross."

"She couldn't have gotten far."

Emmie reached her car first, but Finn rushed past it back toward the house. "I need to get something," he said. A minute later, he emerged from the front door cradling his Beast.

Emmie climbed into the driver's seat and waited for him to get in before starting the car.

"We might need this." He patted the top of the device. "And, by the way, the book is gone too. The French occult book."

"Josephine must need it for something other than releasing Victor—we've learned the hard way that removing the cross does that much. I'm sure her plans for revenge go further than we know."

Pulling out of the driveway, Emmie couldn't help but imagine the suffering Sarah must be going through. Her grandmother's death, Betty's death, and now this. She squeezed the steering wheel while clenching her teeth as she sped off toward the cemetery. "If Josephine hurts her..."

"I'm right there with you." Finn searched the road and fields as Emmie sped up. "I didn't even hear her leave the house. Where were you?"

Emmie met his eyes for a moment. "Trapped in Betty's basement."

Finn's eyes widened. "You broke into her house?"

"She slipped me a key before she died. I had to find out what it belonged to. And I'm glad I did. There's a ton of info down there about her past and the occult and... my parents."

"Oh?"

"I didn't have time to read much. I separated stuff to bring and had to leave it behind, so I'll need to go back, after we get Josephine under control."

No sign of Sarah during their drive to the cemetery. Emmie groaned. "Sarah must have beat us there."

"What if we're too late?" Finn asked.

Emmie didn't want to think about it. "We're not," she answered without confidence.

But when the cemetery came into view, there was still no sign of Sarah. Instead of going inside through the front gate, Emmie parked the car half a block away, behind a line of pine trees. If Sarah/Josephine was already there, it might help to conceal their arrival. It was clear that Josephine was capable of doing anything, so it was important to approach Sarah with caution.

Emmie switched off the engine just as Sarah appeared ahead, moving through the cemetery trees with her head down and holding something to her chest. The book. She had beaten them there.

"There she is." Emmie pointed and scrambled out of the car.

Emmie ran toward the nearest section of cemetery fence, but Finn directed her a little further down.

"This way. There's a gap ahead where we can slip through."

They passed through the opening and weaved between trees and gravestones toward Sarah.

What's the plan? What *was* their plan? Emmie had never pushed spirits; that was Sarah's skill, and there wasn't time to prepare anything new. The best they could hope for was to restrain Sarah and get her away from Josephine without anyone getting hurt, but even that would be a miracle.

Help! she pleaded inside. Her body tensed, bracing for the confrontation.

Fortunately, the cemetery was empty. Rushing toward Victor's grave, they circled a group of trees and spotted Sarah not too far ahead. They still had time to stop her.

"I'll distract her," Emmie said, "then you run up behind her and grab her."

Finn gave her a look that said, *Really?* But it was all she had, and thankfully he didn't question her.

Emmie crept forward while Finn circled behind her. Sarah's eyes were open, but her stare didn't waver from her target ahead: Victor's grave. The grass and creaking branches swaying in the breeze overhead muffled her footsteps. Emmie held back the impulse to run to her friend and embrace her like a parent rushing to rescue a child in danger, but the experience in Betty's basement was still vivid in her mind. *This isn't Sarah.*

After Finn positioned himself and nodded to Emmie, she stepped closer and called out, "Sarah!" No more advantage of surprise.

Together they moved in from both sides, Finn still gripping his Beast device in one hand.

"Josephine," Emmie yelled, "let go of Sarah."

Instead, Josephine met Emmie's eyes with a grin as she continued toward the grave. "So nice of you to join me for this reunion with Victor, but don't even think of interfering. I control the empath. You saw what happens to those who get in my way."

"Just leave Sarah alone."

"She is being useful."

"She's not some toy to play with."

"Nor am I. You need to learn your place. You're dealing with someone with skills far beyond your own. A little too much interference from you and I will carve your name on one of those gravestones at your feet."

Still keeping pace with Josephine, Emmie focused on the spirit within Sarah. She pictured the beautiful red-haired woman standing in front of her. She couldn't push Josephine from Sarah, but she could call her away as her parents had taught her. With her eyes partially closed, the outline of Josephine's spirit encompassing Sarah appeared like an aura. The reddish-blue colors clashed and flared.

Emmie pulled harder.

Josephine screamed and stopped a few yards from reaching Victor's grave. Her muscles tensed, and she scowled at Emmie.

"Don't waste my time." Josephine clenched her fists. *"Partez!"*

Meditate and communicate. Emmie pulled at Josephine's spirit, and for a moment they separated, with Josephine's upper torso angling out forward as if Sarah were birthing a woman from her chest. The colors shifted and intensified.

Finn caught the book that fell from her hand and placed it on the ground with the Beast, then jumped forward and grabbed Sarah's arms. She fought against him for a few seconds and took in several quick breaths before collapsing.

Sarah twisted around toward him, her eyes fluttering back to life. "Finn? What's happening to me? Help me."

"We're trying." Finn held on to Sarah's arms. "Pull away from Josie if you can. Come on, honey."

Sarah was herself for only a moment longer before Josephine's spirit snapped back into her body. Emmie strained to pull her out again, but now she was met with a wall of dark energy that saturated the air between them.

Extending her hands toward Emmie, Sarah curled her fingers into claws. This was Josephine, and it was clear she would strangle Emmie if she broke free from Finn. "You will regret your actions. *Allez droit à l'enfer!*"

"If anyone's going to hell, it's you," Finn said, holding on so hard he was gritting his teeth.

An invisible weight pounded into Emmie's body, thrusting her back over a knee-high gravestone. She spun around before crashing onto the mercifully soft grass of the cemetery. Her legs stretched out and her hands snapped across her chest as if pulled in by magnets until the world stopped and she stared up into the tree branches and churning, darkening clouds. The weight held her in place as she shrugged to move her arms or legs. She craned her face toward Josephine.

"Get used to your new position." Josephine's grin spread. "Finn, *mon chéri*, why do you hold me so tight? You have me in your arms once again, and it's so sweet, but you lost your chance to impress me. *Mon petit sot.*" She jabbed her elbows back against his chest, breaking his hold as he cried out in pain before flipping him forward. His head missed the edge of a gravestone by inches.

"That's better."

Sarah rushed to Victor's grave and climbed to the top with all the skill of a mountain climber. Within seconds, she gripped the cross and began to turn it, erupting in laughter as the metal squeaked louder with each twist.

The iron cross broke free in a brilliant flash of light and blasted into the air before crashing down a few seconds later against a nearby gravestone. Josephine held out her arms over Victor's grave and called out, *"Sors de ton trou, diable!"*

Still pinned to the ground, Emmie watched Finn rise and run to his Beast device. He aimed it at Josephine while she chanted in French atop Victor's grave. The device let out a beep and a click before Josephine convulsed and wavered to the side.

"*Non, non, non!*" Josephine shrieked. "This is my moment. Mine! What are you doing to me?"

Finn kept the device aimed at her as he stepped up behind her, standing only a few feet away. Her eyes rolled up into her head and she collapsed, falling down onto the grass with one leg slamming against the base of Victor's grave on the way down.

Sarah!

On the ground, she let out a guttural moan, then rolled to the side and curled into a ball.

Finn glanced at Emmie. "Can you get up?"

Emmie struggled, but the energy holding her in place didn't weaken. "No."

Sarah's body lay shuddering, as if Finn had stuck her finger in an outlet.

"What do I do?" Finn asked.

Emmie opened her mouth to answer, but Sarah stopped moving as a dark form escaped her body, still shaking within the focus of Finn's device. The form changed in that moment, in the blink of an eye, into a man she'd never seen before. The left side of the man's head was a gaping, bloody wound.

Finn lowered his device and stood staring at the man. "Neil?"

As Finn stepped toward him, Emmie's heart raced. "It's a trick, Finn."

Finn's brother approached him smiling, arms wide. "Yes, it's me, you idiot..."

"Why did you do it, Neil?"

"It wasn't your fault. Of course I'll tell you. I love you."

Finn raised the Beast again, while switching it back on, and aimed it at his brother. "That is definitely not something Neil would say."

Neil convulsed within the device's energy and transformed back into the familiar red-haired woman dressed in white.

"I've got her," Finn said.

Josephine inched toward Finn now, with her hands stretched toward his throat.

The energy holding Emmie down diminished, then disappeared. She scrambled to stand and rushed over to Sarah first—she was breathing, but she didn't respond when Emmie called her name.

"Get the cross back up there," Finn said, struggling now to hold Josephine in place.

Emmie nodded and retrieved the cross, which had landed several feet away. The bottom was partly melted, but maybe it would still fit, at least to hold the spirit until they figured out what to do. She had another cross like that back at Caine House, after all. She scaled the side of Victor's grave with a lot more difficulty than Josephine had.

"I'm almost there!"

Too late.

A sneering, black-haired man in an old-fashioned suit stood a few feet away. There was no mistaking the face she'd seen in the portraits on most walls of the haunted house.

Victor Caine.

❧ 32 ❧

Victor didn't speak at first. His gaze jumped from Finn to Emmie, and then down to Sarah. "Who are you? I don't know your faces..." He stared at Josephine. "... but you... Is that my treacherous French doll?"

Josephine silently clenched her fists and sneered.

Victor grinned. "Josephine, your scowl is still as endearing as I remember it, but how did you rise again? I'm sure you were quite dead only yesterday. I laid you to rest with my own hands, *mon amour*."

Josephine groaned, still frozen within the grasp of Finn's device. "I will do the same for you, Victor. With my own hands."

"You said those same words the last time we spoke, didn't you? But look at you now. This fine gentleman is not even struggling, but it looks like he holds the great witch in the palm of his hand. What magic has captured you like a wounded animal in a fur trap?"

Victor glanced at Finn, but didn't wait for him to answer before continuing. "Whatever it is, I approve. This one is not to be taken lightly, and she does not look happy at all in her present state." He laughed and studied Finn's device.

Finn's face was white. "Emmie... I can see him."

"I know. He's pretty solid."

"What should I do?"

"Nothing yet." Truth was, she had no idea.

Victor narrowed his eyes and stepped closer to Josephine. "What are you thinking now, my dear, that you'll overcome me this time? I locked you in your grave before, and I can put you back."

Josephine clenched her teeth, but her tone softened, and she forced a smile. "Finn, *mon chéri,* step aside. You are not thinking with a clear head. Victor cannot be allowed to go free. I am the only one who can control him."

Emmie met Finn's gaze. "Don't listen to her."

A flurry of sounds erupted in the air around Victor's grave. Men's grumbling voices, and the rustling of boots and leather. Footsteps approached from all sides until five cloudy forms settled in beside Victor.

"I can see them too." Finn's eyes widened, but he held the Beast steady.

One balding man wore a respectable business suit like Victor and a top hat, and his face was dark purple. White foam seeped from his mouth, and he didn't speak. Emmie guessed he had died by poison.

An older man wore a soldier's uniform and carried a rifle with a bayonet attached at the end. His jaw was gone, and shredded chunks of loose flesh hung from his upper mouth. A self-inflicted gun blast?

Two others had identical facial features. Brothers? They wore prairie-farmer clothes: pants held up with suspenders, long-sleeve white cotton shirts, scarves around their necks, and cowboy hats. They carried revolvers and holsters at their hips, and had holes through their chests—straight through the heart.

The fifth man wore darker clothes and had a deep stare; a sheriff's badge was pinned to his chest. The spurs on his leather boots jingled when he moved, and a wide, thick mustache obscured his mouth, but his frown was clear and menacing. His head wobbled a bit, exposing the red rope mark over his throat.

Looking down at his spurs, Finn said, "It's definitely them, Emmie. The ghosts from Caine House."

The sheriff mumbled to Victor in a garbled tone—broken words—but Victor seemed to understand him.

"Don't you worry about a thing, Jack." Victor stepped behind Finn toward the sheriff. "I'm here now. This town is under control again, and it's going to stay that way."

"We waited for you at the house, sir," the man with the uniform said.

"Like a good soldier." Victor turned to one of the brothers and straightened the man's hat. "I hope you didn't turn it into a whorehouse while I was away."

The younger brother mumbled, "No, sir, but we looked for you everywhere. Where did you go?"

Victor's expression changed to a blank stare over the man's shoulder. "I didn't go anywhere. Just fell asleep, is all."

The older brother gestured to Emmie, Finn, and then Sarah. "These folks moved into your house. We tried to get them out, but they didn't listen to us for nothing."

"Trespassers." Victor grumbled. "That's breaking the law, and nothing I hate worse in this town than lawbreakers. We'll hang them from the trees."

The men straightened up, nodded, and grinned.

Stepping over to Sarah, Victor stared down at her. He kicked her shoulder lightly with her boot. "This one drunk?"

Emmie pulled Sarah away. "She needs help. Josephine did this to her."

"See," Victor said, "you can't trust that woman with anything. Evil from the day I met her."

"Release me, Finn," Josephine screeched again. *"Mais laisse-moi!"*

Victor ignored her completely and focused on Emmie now. He stared into her eyes, and his face changed slowly as the uncomfortable moment dragged on. The corner of his upper lip rose as his eyes narrowed. "I know who you are. You have the same frightened, naïve, white face as a woman who came to kill me. But I dealt with her, so she must be... your mother?" An understanding spread across his face and he sneered a little. "Oh, I see. Your mother and father thought they could ruin me, take away all I've worked for, but they got what they deserved."

"What did you do to them?" Emmie demanded.

"Don't you know I will do whatever it takes to stop anyone from spreading lies about me? I expect you plan to spread lies about me too."

The younger brother laughed. "I think she'll be lying about lying when she answers that."

"Plenty of trees here, boss." The soldier tilted the bayonet at the end of his rifle toward Emmie. "We could hang her up now."

"Good thinking, Billy." Victor sneered, moving within inches of Emmie's face, still glaring into her eyes. "And you thought the witch would help you. But she only cares about herself."

Emmie didn't answer. She shook Sarah's shoulder. *We've got a big problem.* Sarah's eyes fluttered.

"We only came here to stop Josephine," Finn shouted.

"More lies!" the sheriff yelled back.

"Stop the French witch from doing what? Killing me? I have no doubt she intends to finish me off, but she won't get the chance. Everything she says is a fabrication. Her lips are as sweet as wine, but when her tongue gets working, only the most foul words escape. She's probably already filled your heads with tales of deceit, and I know you will spread those lies if I let you go. I can't let that happen, not in the town I built with my dreams and my sweat."

"We aren't here to destroy you, Victor," Emmie said.

"No point in taking a chance. Billy's right—you've got to hang."

Emmie didn't see any rope with the men, only the weapons in their hands and holsters, but her heart beat faster anyway.

They couldn't kill her with those weapons, could they? The Hanging Girl had strangled Emmie in the basement. She had *felt* Alice Hyde's hands grip her throat, and she had almost lost consciousness. But how far could these men go? Could they really kill her?

"You've got it wrong. We're here to help you," Emmie said. "All of you."

Victor pushed closer to Emmie. "Liar! That witch, your mother, tried to take me down, and I won. I always win. You're here for the same thing. I can see it in your eyes. That same vulturous look to ruin me and take my wealth. They ran like chickens in their horseless carriage, but I chased them down and destroyed them before they could ruin my name. They didn't get away, and neither will you."

❦ 33 ❦

As Victor inched closer, Emmie stumbled back. His words echoed in her mind, and her heart ached at the realization that this spirit had somehow killed her parents.

The car crash.

A sickening nausea spread through her. Anger and hatred warmed her face, aimed at Victor, but also at herself.

Some stupid thief had stolen the cross from Victor's grave and her parents had risked their lives to return it—to put Victor back in his cage before more innocents died in Lake Eden at his hands. Her parents had done the right thing, but it had cost them their lives. They were too weak to handle such a powerful spirit.

Am I strong enough to face him? Her mother had always told her that she had more power than anyone she'd ever met—if only she had learned to harness it.

Had she learned enough? The question hung in her mind as Victor's eyes darkened.

"You should not have come here." Victor leaned in toward her. "Did you think you could avenge your parents' death or drag me to justice? Not even my foolish occult mistress could stop me. You won't stand in my way, either. I will silence your tongue forever."

Victor's stature was intimidating, especially the way he leaned forward, towering over her as he spoke. He clenched his hands into fists at his side.

She'd faced so many spirits in her life, but now it was different. Not just shadowy, ethereal presences—these spirits appeared as flesh and blood.

Victor twisted the handle of a dagger in the sheath at his waist. Emmie tensed. Was it possible for a spirit's weapon to kill a living person? Would a bullet from the ghosts' guns still fire and travel through her? That couldn't be, could it?

All that her parents had pushed her through during her childhood now made a lot more sense. They had been preparing her for just such a confrontation, and she had nowhere to run, no one to help her. Even with Sarah's aid, it would be so hard to force these spirits to move on, and now she lay unconscious on the ground.

"Emmie," Finn said, "The battery's draining fast in this thing. Ten percent left."

Josephine let out a wild laugh, finally earning a look from Victor. "Watch out, gentlemen, watch out... I'm coming for you."

Think, Em.

If only she had more time to think it over and plan, but there wasn't time. They were here now, and their faces showed no ounce of mercy or patience.

She could focus and pull in some spirits from nearby, crowd the area so they could make their escape in the chaos. She meditated and half-closed her eyes. Not so easy to focus now, with death facing them. And she had always focused on one spirit in particular, never sent out a random cry for help.

One person came to mind. Betty. Without a pause, she focused on the old woman.

Josephine started laughing. "I know what you're doing, but

you're wasting your time. The old woman is gone, in so many ways."

Her words broke Emmie away from the meditation. Their eyes met for a moment.

"What did you do to her?" Emmie asked.

Josephine chuckled. "She can't help you. Better to just let me take care of Victor myself."

Emmie shut her eyes, meditating again, and more faces appeared. Her parents' spirits must be nearby. Emmie resisted calling out to them. They had already died once by Victor's hand. She couldn't do it.

When she opened her eyes, Victor had taken another step forward.

He raised the dagger he'd pulled out and extended it toward her neck. "You can't outrun me." The blade glistened in the setting sun.

Sarah shifted in the grass and groaned.

Emmie dropped to her side. "Sarah, are you okay? You need to get up now."

Again, Josephine laughed. "Even if she can hear you, she is powerless, and you shouldn't expect her to survive. It won't be long now, unless you free me."

Emmie glanced back to see Victor leaning down, holding the knife closer toward her neck. She shook Sarah's shoulders. "Please wake up."

"I can't keep this going," Finn warned.

Emmie tried again to revive Sarah. If she could just get her up and focused, they would have a chance.

She turned back to Victor, who towered over her now with death in his eyes. "Whatever you did, we don't know anything about it."

"*I do,*" a small voice broke through the tension.

The silhouette several yards away caught Emmie's eye. A boy stood hovering beside a gravestone, his face full of fear.

David.

34

David shielded himself behind the headstone, but he drew himself up when he spoke, pointing at Victor. "He killed my family, and these other men helped him."

Victor stopped and turned toward the boy, his face flushed red. "Do you see that boy, Josephine? You told me all of them were locked in place, but at least one escaped. Apparently, you are not the occult master you thought you were. Or did you do this on purpose? Leaving a witness behind."

Josephine's eyes narrowed. "The boy's body must not have been buried with the others. That incompetence belongs to you and your men. But does one child's soul frighten you? Then imagine your terror when dozens of massacred, vengeful souls tear yours apart. You won't escape their judgment."

Emmie focused on the boy. "David, can you help us? Are there other victims nearby?"

"Yes, David, please run and get help," Josephine said. "Gather all who were murdered and bring them here so they can drag Victor away. Here's your chance to deliver justice for your slain family and avenge their deaths. Wouldn't that be a most delightful sight?

"I'm alone." David's eyes watered. "I can't find my family."

"Finn, I can free all the murdered innocents and bring them here to finish this," Josephine said.

Victor laughed. "Oh, so you wish to play the part of a savior now? You locked them in their graves! My witch, you would have astounded the crowds as an actress."

Victor's cronies laughed. "Slit her throat again," the sheriff cried.

Josephine's spirit struggled against Finn's device. "Finn, you're making a mistake. Free me this instant before he gets away. These men murdered entire families, and we can bring them to justice today."

The twins in Victor's group broke off and stalked toward David as he backed away.

"Emmie," Finn said with growing alarm.

Victor and the remaining three men shifted and closed in. "Silence them," Victor commanded, slicing his dagger through the air and extending it toward Emmie's throat. "Hang them or cut their throats, I don't care which."

Emmie stared at the blade, now only an arm's length away.

Victor lunged forward, and the tip of the dagger slashed across Emmie's arm. The pain was sharp and immediate. He beamed with a wild, empty stare that chilled her blood. The dagger felt real, and if she couldn't defend herself now, someone would find her body in the grass the next day.

"No!" Finn yelled. "Emmie, run!"

Emmie met Finn's eyes for a moment. "Switch it off. Let her go."

Finn hesitated for a moment, then powered it off.

Josephine burst forward at Victor with a frightening fury and slammed him back several feet while his men scrambled to get out of the way. The dagger flew from his hand as she clawed at his throat.

Finn pulled Emmie back, and they gathered beside Sarah.

Emmie pressed her hand to Sarah's forehead. Ice cold, but still unconscious. "We need to get her out of here."

"Agreed." Finn handed his device to Emmie, aiming it toward Victor's cohort, who attempted to surround them. He reached in and switched it back on for her, and the men froze in place, struggling to raise their weapons. "I'll take her."

Emmie blocked Finn as he pulled Sarah up. "Hurry, Finn."

Josephine gained the upper hand over Victor, holding him in place despite her smaller frame, while reciting some French phrases that appeared to weaken him. She knocked him to the ground and his eyes glazed over as if caught in a trance. His muscles relaxed, and she leaned forward with a devious grin. "Revenge is mine, Victor."

Without warning, Finn's device shut down. No more power. Victor's men lurched toward them, but the sheriff stopped them, staring over at Victor.

"Get her off Victor," the sheriff ordered.

The men complied and tackled Josephine before she could defend herself. The sheriff grabbed Josephine, cupping his hand over her mouth while the soldier clutched her hair and neck.

A little dazed, Victor stood up and stepped to Josephine, grumbling out a few French phrases of his own. Grabbing his iron cross from the ground, he recited the French louder as he pressed it against her breast. The man in uniform unwrapped a sash from his waist and hurried forward to tie the cross in place. Josephine's eyes softened and her body relaxed as if wavering on the edge of sleep.

"Is this what you had in mind for me, my dear?" Victor grinned as he tightened the sash. "To weigh me down with iron and throw me in the darkness with the settlers, like a cat trapped in a cage with a thousand hungry dogs? You can't destroy me or my name. The settlers know very well who locked them in limbo, and their rage won't discriminate between you and me— they'll rip you apart, my pathetic witch."

Victor dragged her toward the cemetery's entrance like a hunter dragging home a kill before the feast, and his men followed along behind him, leaving Emmie, Sarah, and Finn behind as if they didn't matter. As Victor and his men left, their bodies dissolved into shadows.

"Thank God, they're gone." Finn stopped struggling to lift Sarah to her feet. Now he lowered her and kneeled beside her. "Sarah, wake up, girl."

"He'll come back for us." Emmie moved up beside Sarah across from Finn.

Finn met Emmie's eyes, then turned his attention back to Sarah. Each of them tried desperately to revive her.

Emmie wiped the hair from Sarah's face. "Oh, God, Finn, she's not breaking out of it."

Finn scooped up the French book. "Is there anything in here that might undo what Josephine did to Sarah?"

A sense of powerlessness and failure washed over Emmie. "I don't know. We just didn't have time enough to study it."

"Let's get her back to the car. We should take her to the hospital."

Sarah's eyes half opened then, and her gaze shifted from Finn to Emmie. Her mouth moved, but no words came out.

"Yes, Sarah?" Emmie asked, moving her ear in closer to Sarah's mouth. "Stay with us."

David now came out from behind the gravestone, where he had hidden during the confrontation, and walked over to them, standing only a few feet away. He stared at Sarah. "Is she going to die?"

Emmie squeezed Sarah's shoulder. "No."

"Did they get away?"

Emmie swallowed. "For now. My friend needs help. We need to get her to the hospital."

"They're going to hurt my family again, aren't they?"

"No, David. They're safe, for the moment."

"Sometimes I hear my mother crying out, from far away."

"We'll help her, I promise." Emmie gently shook Sarah. "Sarah, can you hear me?"

She gave a subtle nod and shifted.

Emmie held her hand under Sarah's shoulder. "We're going to take you to the hospital."

Sarah tilted her head, just a little, and moved it from side to side.

"No? Are you sure?" Emmie looked at Finn. An idea had occurred to her because of David. "I think I know how to stop them, Victor and Josephine."

"Shouldn't we just let them go?" he asked. "They'll destroy themselves, right?"

"Each intends to trap the other in with the victims, but this would only make things worse, as one of them will win and be free to raise hell. He's more powerful than Josephine, and after he's done with her, we'll be the ones standing in his way. I've seen what happened to Lake Eden the last time someone removed his cross—it was like an apocalypse here—and it'll be a lot worse this time unless we stop him. We need to get to the Monument to the Innocents first and release their souls, before Victor and Josephine can do any more damage."

"That'll make them *both* pissed at us. And my Beast is dead."

"Bring along the French book." Emmie searched for Victor's dagger, but it was gone. *It never existed?* But the cut on her arm proved the danger was real.

"How can we stop them this time?" Finn asked.

"We'll figure that out when we get there. But I'm sure the victims need to be released, and if we can wake Sarah, we can stop them."

"Can you force souls like Victor and Josephine to move on?"

"If you can call them souls... devils, more like it. I guess we'll find out." She turned to Sarah. "What do you think, girl, does that sound like a plan?"

A subtle nod from Sarah and Emmie's heart lightened. She glanced at David. "Can you wait back at the cornfield? I'll come for you after it's safe."

He shook his head. "I want to stay with you."

"All right."

They moved Sarah along, each lifting one side. Sometimes Sarah took a step, but it more resembled the gait of an incoherent drunk.

Finn tried to carry the Beast with them, but discarded it in the grass along the way. "The thing's dead anyway. It served us well, I guess. I'll just pick it up later. Who's going to take it?"

Victor, his men, and Josephine were nowhere in sight as they left the cemetery. It wouldn't take them long to get to the Monument to the Innocents.

With Sarah in the passenger seat and Finn in the back of the car, Emmie rushed across town. So much was at stake this time, there wasn't time to lose.

"Get that occult book ready," Emmie said to Finn. "And get fluent in French. You've got five minutes."

35

Emmie had never visited the Monument to the Innocents before, but she'd heard about it. Not a place to go for psychics like her. So many desperate voices would cry out to her as soon as she arrived—dozens had been murdered there—and for someone who'd only begun to face her fears this was, as Betty had said, like being thrown into the deep end of the pool.

Finn directed her to the monument. It sat at the opposite end of the lake, not more than a couple of miles from Caine House, beside the county road that ran into town. Anxiety spread through her chest as she turned into the driveway intended for temporary roadside visits and then followed another branching road circling behind it to a small park. A single light on a pole near the road lit the monument, but the park was empty and dark. A car passed by after she pulled in—if they had noticed her, they didn't slow down.

The memorial looked exactly as she'd seen it in pictures during her school years. Just a slab of granite, a few feet high and wide, with a few lines of inscriptions carved across the front. Two pine trees stood beside the memorial like noble guards, which helped to obscure the picnic area behind it. Beyond the edge of the area was the vast complex of Caine Industries.

"I didn't see a cross on the memorial," Emmie said. "And I don't see Victor or Josephine either—or anyone." Emmie parked in one of the spots along the far back edge, as far away from the main road as she could get. "Are you sure this is where the massacre happened?"

"The granite memorial out front was constructed recently—within the last fifty years, according to what I've discovered. Something for the tourists to view and read, but there's an old grave marker back there. I'll show you." Finn gestured to the far corner of the park.

The headlights glared ahead for a moment. Not much there. No attractive features like a playground or a great view of the lake, just a few barbecue pits, and a wall of pine trees separating the park from the Caine Industries property. A rest area with nothing to do but contemplate the massacre.

"Then where are they?" Emmie asked.

Finn pushed his door open. "Maybe we beat them."

"I'm sure it won't be long before they arrive."

"How fast can a ghost travel, anyway?"

"I don't know. I guess we'll find out." Emmie turned to Sarah. "Are you doing okay?"

She nodded with her face down. "Better."

Together they helped Sarah out of the car and took her over to the back of the picnic area. If what Josephine had said was true about the trapped souls of the settlers, and if Sarah had recovered enough, they could immediately begin to make things right.

"The grave marker is over here." Finn led them further into the darkness, switching on his cellphone to light the way.

"We'll need to release their spirits first."

"Ready when you are," he said, taking the French occult book and sticking it in the back of his waistband.

Branches brushed against Emmie's arms as they pushed through the pine trees. "How far is it?"

"Not far. Behind these trees."

Emmie caught her shoe against something protruding from the ground, and stumbled forward with a shriek. Finn caught her, and they all glanced back at the object nearly buried behind a thick growth of grass. It stood out now with Finn's cellphone providing extra light.

It was a stone marker laying flush against the ground. Nothing grand about it—just a simple flat stone with the symbol of a bird carved across its face. No names, dates, or explanation. The symbol was oddly familiar.

"I didn't see that one before," Finn said, continuing on his original path. "But the thing we're looking for is right... there." His cellphone lit up a stone memorial several feet high. The stone was weathered and chipped away in many places, as if someone had used it for target practice—maybe someone had. It towered over them, tapering at the top, with dozens of stars etched into its sides. "Fifty-seven stars for all the victims."

"Should be fifty-eight. They missed little David."

At the top of the tower sat the black cross with French wording on the front. The same wording as on the ones at Victor's and Josephine's graves.

"This is it." Finn inched forward.

"Okay. We'll need to remove the cross first and free them, then go back and use the French words to lock the worst spirits again, Victor, his men and Josephine."

"This might be a little tricky, even if we are right and the passage is the one that was marked. But let's go by stages."

Finn pulled out the French book and his phone, then handed them to Emmie as he walked to the base of the grave marker and studied the sloping sides. "Don't know if I'll be as good a climber as Josephine, but here goes."

Grabbing the corners, he scaled the monument, lifting himself a few inches at a time. His shoes squeaked against the weathered granite, and his arms strained to hang on, but he made it to the top within a minute. With his hands gripping the cross, he glanced back at Emmie. "Ready?"

She nodded once.

"Be careful," Sarah called out.

He began turning the cross, as he'd done before. With each spin, he leaned a little further back, keeping his face turned away. Before he was through, the cross snapped off and exploded into the air with a white flash of light.

It blinded Emmie for a moment, and she covered her eyes until her sight returned.

"Holy shit." Finn slid down the side of the memorial quickly as the cross crashed to the ground, cracking against several pine branches along the way.

Emmie stepped back and Sarah staggered closer, then silence filled the air. Some birds fluttered away in the darkness, and Finn dropped to the grass below.

He gasped for breath. "So, where are they?"

"I feel them." Sarah moaned. "Oh my God. It's awful. All of them are coming out and it's so painful!"

"There they are." Emmie's body chilled. Dozens of spirits moved up around them, sprouting like trees. All of them showed ghastly wounds over their bodies from gunshots and knives. Men, women, and children—the murderers had shown no mercy and had taken down every one brutally. Their cries escalated as they rose. All that Emmie had feared now surrounded her as they circled in around her begging for justice. They pleaded with her to find their brothers, sisters, mothers, fathers, sons, and daughters.

Finn glanced around. "I don't see them."

"Consider yourself lucky." She tried to back away, but they came in from every side.

Sarah moved between her friend and the spirits, reaching out blindly to find the closest one, and pushing her hands through the spirit. Within seconds, the spirit transformed into light and rose in the air before its presence dispersed like a wisp of glowing smoke and then disappeared.

Despite the growing desire to push them away, Emmie

focused on them, pulling them in closer instead so that Sarah might release them faster, even without being able to see them. She couldn't leave any of them behind with Victor and Josephine on the way.

"What's happening?" Finn asked.

"They are here, and Sarah is helping them on," Emmie cried.

Finn raised his face to the sky.

Sarah released crying, panicked children and desperate parents, all of them reliving the terror that had occurred on that spot at Victor's hands until they found peace.

A short time later, with just a few victims left, Finn's voice broke the air. "They're here."

Sarah continued without pausing, but Emmie followed Finn's gaze back to the parking lot where the shadows of Victor and Josephine had taken solid form again, along with Victor's five accomplices.

"You'll pay for violating my land," Victor growled, dragging Josephine behind him, still burdened by the cross strapped to her chest.

Josephine shrieked, staring at Sarah as she released one of the last souls. "What are you doing? You're letting them go? Are you crazy? How will they have their revenge? Victor will get away with it!"

Finn moved beside Emmie, blocking Sarah as Victor, his men, and Josie approached. "They need peace."

"You're wrong, *espèce d'idiot*! They need to rip his soul apart."

Emmie looked back as Sarah finished releasing the last victim, a frail teen girl in a white dress with blood eternally streaking down over her chest. The girl gazed into Emmie's eyes before dispersing, a bewildered stare at first that transformed into joy before she faded away.

"Too late," Emmie said with a tired smile.

🦋 36 🦋

After the spirits of the settlers had passed on, they stood side-by-side as Victor and his cohort approached, dragging Josephine along beside them. An energy filled the air like a bristling static before a storm that causes one's hair to stand on end.

Emmie prepared for the confrontation in the only way she could—by taking in deep breaths and clearing her mind. The heaviness in her chest wouldn't stop her from facing their imminent wrath for releasing the spirits of the settlers, but she only wished she could face the vile spirits alone to spare her friends from any harm. But hadn't that been her parents' fatal mistake? To face Victor alone? This was how it should be—the three of them, together—and just like Betty had said, "Together, they could be dangerous."

I hope more dangerous than the spirits are.

Josephine's face reflected her fury, with bared teeth and a piercing stare that struck at Emmie's confidence. No doubt, Josephine would have destroyed all of them in a moment, if she only had the chance. Victor gripped Josephine by the neck, and the woman's arms thrashed as they approached.

Victor's presence chilled the late summer air. He sneered

while walking beside his entourage, although their feet never touched the ground. His gaze fell on each of them, but he was silent.

Josephine cried out, seemingly more upset by the release of the victims' souls than by Victor's assault. "You will burn in hell along with Victor for what you've done. The settlers cried out for revenge, and you denied them."

His expression changed, and he let out a gruff laugh. "You should rejoice, my dear, as they've rescued you from the feeding frenzy that would have torn your soul apart. But fortunately, I have other ways to make you suffer. Shall I lock you in your grave again?"

"C'est moi qui va te détruire!" Josephine struggled within Victor's grasp, screaming more French words that Emmie assumed were curses by the woman's snarls, then spat at his face as dark clouds formed around Victor's head like claws. The thin, boney fingers stretched out and covered Victor's eyes.

"What's this?" Victor brushed away the hands as if he were swatting flies, but Josephine thrust backwards and wiggled a little further from his grasp. "You won't take me down that easily."

He yanked her hair to pull her in closer now as the shadowy form dissipated, then clamped his hand over her mouth. "Locking you in your grave might not be enough to keep you silent. You need far worse. How would you go about that, my sly witch? What dark French magic might I use to put you away forever? I learned many things from you during our years together, French, magic, and some nice tricks in bed. But the most valuable lesson was to stay one step ahead—something you failed to do, or you wouldn't be in this predicament now."

"You haven't taken me down yet. Are the dark powers you cherish so much enough to fill the void of your hollow heart?"

"My Pa always told me emotions were for the weak. Pity, charity, love... they all cloud judgement, but I never let them cloud mine. You're an emotional woman, poor witch, so you couldn't help yourself, and you lost the game."

"Your Pa," Josephine cackled. "Who was he, Satan himself?"

"What was the phrase from your book again? Ah, yes... *Enfants des ténèbres, drainez la lumière de la terre et acceptez le sacrifice que je jette dans le sein éternel du mal...*"

"No, Victor." Josephine struggled and cried out. "You can't do this to me."

He laughed. "I am doing it."

Josephine turned to Finn, stretching out her hand. "Help me, Finn. Victor cannot stop us if we work together, but we need to act now. Free me from this cross!"

Victor laughed as Finn hesitated, held back by Emmie. "The boy doesn't want you either. We'll both celebrate when your spirit is crushed."

A wind circled around them, kicking up the leaves and dirt. Emmie shivered and stepped back, holding Sarah behind her. Finn turned away from Josephine but glanced at her over his shoulder. The wind grew stronger, whipping around them as if a tornado had caught them. A dark opening formed on the ground near Josephine's feet. A void that spread wider and consumed the grass and debris around it like a black hole. As it spread apart, a thick sulfur stench filled the air.

"What the hell?" Finn cried, protecting his friends with his body as they looked, wide-eyed, at the scene before him.

"Victor, stop before it's too late." Josephine thrashed like a fish caught on a hook.

"It's too late for you, my dear. Do you see their faces coming for you?"

The shadows within the void moved. Emmie saw their eyes first, then their fingers and twisted, ghastly expressions. Demons? Lost spirits? The first one rose from the spinning hole that now spread several feet wide and lashed out at Victor's entourage, slashing its fingers over the sheriff's boots.

Victor dangled Josephine near the edge. "Feast on her."

Josephine shrieked. "You've opened the gates of hell now to rid yourself of me?"

"If they'll accept you."

She clawed her way back into Victor's arms and broke free for a moment, scrambling to escape the vortex intensifying beneath her. The spirits within the hole sprang up like wild beasts, attacking any who stood nearby, then sank back into the darkness before pouncing again. Something unseen tethered them to the darkness.

The five men blocked Josephine's escape. Each of the twins grabbed one of her arms and the soldier and businessman grabbed her legs. They dragged her to the edge again and tried to heave her in, but a dark spirit rose from the hole and snaked its claws around the soldier's leg, pulling him into the darkness kicking and screaming. The other four men rushed to rescue him, fighting to keep Josephine down at the same time.

Her gaze bypassed Finn this time, shining with an unearthly blue light, and fell on Sarah. *"C'est à toi!"*

Sarah stared back, her eyes also shining bright for a moment, and Finn turned away as Josephine slipped closer to the hole.

"She's not alive," Emmie reminded him. "She's been gone a long time."

Victor kicked Josephine back as she attempted to escape, but she clung to the edge. "Let go and enjoy your new eternal home," he said.

As Victor's men dragged Josephine down, a spirit sprang up and clutched her torso. The men let her go as she fought with the dark spirit, but before they could back away, more spirits exploded from the hole and plucked them one by one from the edge. Two spirits twisted their forms over the sheriff's face and neck, then plummeted with him headfirst into the hole.

The twins fought and pleaded with Victor as something within the abyss drew them back. "Help us, Victor!"

Instead of helping them, Victor stepped back.

"Won't you help us?" the businessman pleaded, his eyes wide with terror.

Victor kicked him toward the hole. "Accept your fate and stop your sniveling."

His men disappeared, and screaming erupted before a deafening silence fell seconds later.

Josephine spoke only in French now, crying out in pain as the three spirits pulled at her, then four. Gasping and tearing her fingers against the hole's edge as she slid back, she stared again at Finn. "Your brother is here with me, Finn."

She dropped into darkness.

❧ 37 ❧

Victor turned and gazed from Emmie to Sarah and Finn. "Only three more malicious tongues to silence."

He moved toward them with cold, glassy eyes and clutched Finn by the neck, lifting him into the air a few feet before Finn broke free and crashed to the ground.

Gasping for air, Finn jumped up and hammered his fists into Victor's abdomen.

Victor grinned and swatted Finn's arms away. "Why bother, little man? Wouldn't you rather jump in the hole with Josephine? It seems she's taken a shine to you."

"Not interested."

Victor grabbed both of Finn's wrists and squeezed. "You'd better make your peace, as you will spend eternity together. And she can be delightful."

Finn cried out in pain as his knees buckled and he dropped to the ground. "Son of a bitch!"

Victor's expression lit up even more as he dragged Finn several feet toward the hole.

Sarah and Emmie rushed over to Finn, pulling at his feet as he slid face-down toward the darkness. A few feet from the edge, Victor slowed, and it became a game of tug-of-war with Finn stuck in the middle. He groaned and clenched his teeth while they assured him they wouldn't let go.

A few seconds into the struggle, Sarah slipped and tumbled back, leaving Emmie to keep Finn from falling into the abyss like the others. But instead of getting up, Sarah stayed on the ground and closed her eyes. A serene expression spread over her face.

"Sarah," Emmie called, "what's going on? Finn needs help."

Sarah stared at Victor with a sneer before shouting in a menacing French voice. Josephine's voice. *"Lumière de la terre, je vous invoque! Je vous supplie de contenir tout ce qui est sombre..."*

Victor's reaction was swift. He wavered in place as if caught in a daze, and Finn stopped moving toward the hole. Victor's form became less solid, transforming into a gray gaseous substance that more resembled the traditional ghost. He trembled and strained as if a great pain had shot through him.

The tension in Finn's body loosened a few seconds later, allowing him to break free. He scrambled away, nursing his wrists. "Keep doing that, Sarah! It's working!"

"What did she say?" Emmie asked him.

"Something about calling on the light." Finn scrambled back to Sarah. Her eyes had closed.

The light? Josephine spoke the French words through Sarah, but if the woman was using light to attack Victor, then she must have abandoned her attempts to imprison him again using the dark arts. She was using Sarah's energy to bind him, and her body glowed a deep blue.

Betty's words came back to Emmie. *When certain psychic powers meet, they can complement each other, creating an even greater energy, and energy is what Josephine thrives on.*

Sarah recited another French sentence, and Victor's dark energy vibrated as if a million volts had passed through him.

"She's pushing him now... they are." Emmie stared at Victor's weakened form, but how much time did they have before the struggle would exhaust Sarah?

The French occult book lay on the grass where it had fallen

from Finn's waistband. Emmie scooped it up, but she didn't open it. The Sarah / Josephine combination was holding him, for now, but she fought against the fear that Sarah wasn't strong enough, or that *she* wasn't strong enough.

Her parents had faced the same situation. A sinking feeling passed through Emmie's chest. It had taken a great psychic like Betty to get Victor under control again, but Emmie was no great psychic, and Betty was gone. As she struggled to decide their next step, a boy's voice demanded her attention.

"Emmie?"

Emmie turned to face David. "David? Did you see what happened?"

He nodded.

She stepped toward him, blocking him from Victor's sight. "You need to leave. It's too dangerous with Victor here."

David peered over Emmie's shoulder and scowled at Victor, then gestured back at the Caine Industry property line at the far edge of the picnic area. "They're over there."

"Who?"

"My mom and dad. Thank you for leading me back to them. This is where they died, along with the Sioux who tried to save them. And then I ran into the corn."

Emmie stared into the darkness. Nobody there. "Your parents? We released all the victims."

David's face lit up and rushed toward the Caine Industries property. "I see them!"

Emmie looked back at Sarah, Finn, and Victor. Finn was still crouched beside Sarah with his arm around her. "I don't have time right now, David."

"Yes, there they are!" David yelled.

She focused on him. Blood drained from the hole in his back. "I think your parents are gone."

"No, they're here. Don't you see them?"

Something moved in the darkness ahead. Two forms appeared and stood where David was headed—a man and a woman holding a baby in her arms. He ran over and embraced them while all four spirits glowed.

Emmie stepped toward them, but stopped. They must have stayed behind to wait for their son.

David turned back to Emmie without leaving his parents. "I have to go."

"I understand." Emmie watched as their spirits grew brighter before dissolving as they rose into the air.

What had David said about the Sioux?

The Sioux had tried to save them. From Victor.

Not at all as the town's history had recorded.

So if they, too, were Victor's victims, where were they? Had all the Native Americans already moved on after Victor and his men massacred them? Emmie surveyed the area. No more spirits nearby, but just like David's parents, some could still be out there beyond her sight. Some others could be waiting for the right moment to return.

Perhaps they were waiting for their chance to reveal the truth about what happened. For justice, to clear their name from a foul lie.

Her mind jumped back to the box left behind after her parents' accident. She'd found the French book in there, but also the rune stone... with a symbol carved into it.

She touched her pocket and ran her fingers across the outline of her car keys, and then across the rune stone on her key chain. The stone hadn't mattered before, but now she fumbled to dig it out as fast as she could. Studying the symbol carved in the stone in the light of her cellphone, it made sense—the same symbol as the one on the memorial in front of the picnic area. She'd held the answer with her all along.

Her parents had carried the stone with them when they'd died, but they must not have made the connection to the Sioux. They'd gone to the wrong place using only the French book, and instead of invoking help from the Sioux at the location where they'd died, they had gone straight to Victor's gravesite.

That had been their mistake.

If her parents had only read the French passage to imprison Victor, they wouldn't have been strong enough to control the situation—not by a long shot. They had needed more power.

Shame washed through her. *I should have been there.*

But there wasn't time for self-pity. She focused on the stone in her hand.

Meditate and communicate.

If the Sioux spirits were nearby, then she would pull them in just as she had with all the other massacre victims.

Finn cried out, pulling Emmie out of her trance for a moment. Victor was moving toward Sarah as Finn put himself between, even as Sarah spoke another French sentence. Sarah could push Victor away using the same power she'd used to move spirits on, but it would only work for so long, especially if a spirit this evil didn't want to go. How long could Sarah hold him back before he broke loose again and finished them?

Emmie forced herself to meditate on the Sioux. If she was wrong, they would face the same fate as her parents.

She pushed the thought away and focused harder than she had ever done in her life. The life of her friends was on the line too.

A single, luminous figure appeared against the black backdrop of her eyelids. She opened her eyes to face an old man proudly standing a few feet in front of her. A row of feathers ran along the top of his colorful headband, and three bullet holes drained blood down his chest. Their eyes met and he didn't smile, but Emmie sensed his essence. This was a powerful man with a noble purpose. A shaman, and as he became more solid, he looked up into the sky and raised his arms. The clouds that had swept through earlier in the day formed overhead, blotting out the moon and the stars.

A sudden wind swept through the area as rain pelted the ground. Within minutes, a torrential downpour drenched them as they stood helpless in the soaking grass.

Sarah sat unmoving like a Buddhist statue, while Finn protected her as best he could. Her blue glow faded a little with each inch Victor gained toward her.

The rain poured over Emmie's face, and she gasped for air. The ground rumbled below her feet and the grass shifted, rising like a boat riding a wave on the ocean. She stumbled back as it rose further until the soil exploded, tearing apart the grass as if an unruly creature were trying to escape. The churning water snaked over the area and gushed over the exposed soil, carving a deep crevice that ran hundreds of feet back across the Caine Industries property.

The shaman turned his head toward Caine Industries as a torrent of spirits erupted from where the earth had split apart and from beneath Victor's property. The spirits flew at Victor, enveloping him like a swarm of bees, dimming his spirit, and fought to keep him from advancing toward Sarah or the shaman.

Emmie staggered on her feet, but she refused to leave; within minutes, the rain stopped, fading away as quickly as it had started. The shaman lowered his arms then and led Emmie to a spot where the soil had erupted from the ground. He pointed to the opening, and she followed his gaze. A body lay in the mud, skeletal remains clothed in the same tribal outfit worn by the man with her.

She nodded.

He lowered his head and nodded back, and she knew he wanted her to survive and tell the truth.

Emmie turned back to Victor. He was flailing his arms in his fight against the Sioux spirits as they struck at his spirit. He glared at the shaman, his eyes burning with rage, then he turned back to Sarah, who sat shivering on the ground next to Finn.

The shaman gestured to the book in Emmie's hand. "He is weak. Send him away now."

Drenched from the downpour, Emmie rushed to her friends. "Now, Sarah. Now. He's weak. Stay with me. Say the words."

With Emmie and Finn's help, Sarah struggled to her feet,

took a step forward, and shouted in a voice that was almost her own, "*Lumière de la terre, je vous invoque! Je vous supplie de contenir tout ce qui est sombre...*" She paused and met Emmie's gaze before continuing. Only a faint blue aura remained in her eyes. The last remnants of Josephine. "*Contenez cette âme corrompue et envoyez-la à sa demeure finale! La demeure qu'elle a choisit!*"

With the last word spoken, the ground trembled again, and Victor let out a deep, painful wail as the Sioux spirits surged in. They clutched his arms and legs, then lifted him into the air over the very hole he had opened.

He glared at Emmie before he dropped. His eyes were filled with fear as the creatures within the darkness below him lurched up to pluck him away from the Sioux spirits. His screams filled the air until the hole swallowed him up and closed in on itself.

38

Victor was gone.

And everyone else.

Sarah swayed and stared ahead to where Victor had disappeared. Emmie and Finn each grabbed an arm. She was smiling. "Just give me a minute."

Finn cleared the hair from her face. "Sure."

They released her, but stayed at her side.

She shivered and her teeth chattered. "Is he really gone?"

"Yes, you did it." Emmie touched Sarah's bare arm. "You're freezing. We should get you inside."

"It took a lot out of me."

"I'm sure it did."

Sarah looked at Finn with a smile. "Did I say it right?"

Finn chuckled. "If I didn't know you were reciting an occult phrase, I would have thought your French was incredibly romantic."

Sarah laughed. "Maybe it's time I learn a foreign language to understand what I'm saying."

Emmie looked back to the patch of wet grass that had swallowed up Victor. "It's such a thin wall between us and them. Maybe they'll get out again someday."

"That's why the world needs you." Finn glanced between Sarah to Emmie. "To put everyone where they need to be."

Their attention was drawn to the Native American spirits filing in behind the shaman, who Emmie assumed was their leader. The area soon filled with people of all ages showing the same signs of violent death as the settlers who'd stood there less than half an hour earlier. All of them had suffered and died under Victor's tyranny. Despite their victory, the leader's face was serene. No joy at Victor's demise.

Emmie again nodded at him. "I won't let you down."

The leader turned to face his people and raised his hands again, this time calling out a few words Emmie didn't understand, but their meaning was clear. *Time to go home.*

One by one, their glowing forms ascended into the sky, then flew through the clouds like shooting stars in reverse. The shaman went last.

Police sirens blared in the distance. With everything that had happened around them and an unearthed skeleton only yards away, Emmie motioned for her friends to leave.

Maybe it wasn't a good idea for the police of a small town to question them twice in a couple of days. No signs of foul play, anyway, just a natural disaster that was sure to make headlines in the news tomorrow.

Good. Let them investigate all that Victor did to those people. The unearthed body would jumpstart the discussion. And if they leave anything out, I'll step up and fill in the details.

Finn led them through the trees back to the car. Within a minute, they pulled out of the parking lot and headed back toward Caine House. Passing the blaring police cars along the way, Emmie followed the flashing lights in her rearview mirror as they stormed onto the property of Caine Industries, no doubt the result of the earthquake triggering alarms. Let them figure this all out, if they could.

39

The next morning, Emmie and Sarah gathered up their things and prepared to leave. Finn would be fine by himself now, and all Emmie wanted to do was get back home to the comfort and familiarity of her own bed.

Sarah recovered entirely by morning, even getting up early to make pancakes from scratch for them. They had discussed the events of the previous night wearily, exhausted and yet exhilarated by the fight.

Staying in Victor's mansion had helped expose the truth behind the founder and town hero, but it was up to Lake Eden to decide what to do about his true story. The unearthed shaman's body would lead to questions, and Emmie would make sure the letter she had found in Betty's house got to the authorities.

Finn brandished the letter he had discovered with Victor's own confession of killing Josephine and engaging in dark magic. He smirked and predicted he would not be a favorite with the caretaker for handing it in to the police.

Emmie paused at one of Victor's portraits on the way downstairs. She peered into his eyes and grinned. *You're not so scary now.* Would the caretaker remove Victor's portraits after he learned the murderous truth? Would Caine House's haunted legacy die as the result of what had happened?

"Too many haunted houses," Emmie said as she reached the bottom of the stairs.

"Let's clear them out." Sarah said, laughing where she stood with Finn by the door. "Psychics R Us, right?"

Emmie thought about it, then nodded. "Exactly." It warmed her heart to see Sarah laugh.

"Listen, come over to our place for lunch," Emmie told Finn. "We need a break from Victor's portraits."

"I agree, as long as you promise to order something and not bother with cooking yourself. Let's take it easy today."

"I promise, *mon amour.*"

He both flinched and groaned at the words. "I'll be there."

"Still planning on staying here the full six months?" Sarah asked.

Finn scanned the surrounding walls. "It's an intriguing house. The price will drop further after the news about Victor gets out. Maybe I'll ask if it's for sale."

"You don't seem like the kind of guy to settle down."

He grinned. "We'll see."

They headed out the door, and Emmie didn't look back as she climbed into the car and took off down the road. Approaching the corner before turning left into town, she slowed down and glanced over at Sarah. "I have to do something first."

Sarah understood. "Do you think they will be there?"

"Maybe." Emmie's chest tightened with anxiety. She had never intended to go to the place where her parents had died. Never. But after all she had learned... Things were different now.

Sarah nodded. "I'd like to be with you, then."

"Thank you."

Emmie drove slowly along the gravel road toward the corner where her parents' car had left the road and hit a tree. Butterflies filled her stomach as if she were about to give a speech or go out on a first date.

"I'm afraid," Emmie said.

"Of what?"

"I abandoned them."

"You didn't. It's your mom and dad. They still love you."

"I hope so. I'm ashamed that I judged them and didn't understand."

Emmie pinpointed the curve in the road up ahead and the massive oak just a little further away. *There it is. Mom and Dad died there.*

So would they really have waited years for her to visit?

Scanning the area as she drove closer, she spotted them. Two figures standing beside the road. It was them.

Emmie slowly drove around the curve, all the time imagining her parents taking the same corner at a high speed before they'd crashed. Now she held no resentment or anger, just sadness. She parked along the side of the road, out of the way in case any other cars might pass by during her visit with them.

She met their eyes as she shut off the car's engine. Their faces glowed, both literally and figuratively.

"They're so happy to see you," Sarah said, half closing her eyes and smiling. "They have strong emotions."

"Can you see them?"

"They're coming into view now—becoming solid. They really want to talk with you."

"I'm sure they do," Emmie said softly. "I've got a few things I want to say too."

Sarah unbuckled her seatbelt but didn't get out. "I'll wait here."

Emmie didn't argue. It was better that way. "Thank you."

Her feet scraped against the gravel road as she shuffled toward them. Luckily, there were no farmhouses nearby to witness their encounter.

A smile grew on Emmie's face as she moved forward. The

bitterness of the past—all the things they'd forced her to do: the ghosts, the meditations, the isolation—faded away. They had meant well. It was her parents standing there waiting for her, and pure joy welled up inside her.

They held their arms out, and she did the same.

"My Emmie," her mom said.

"Hi, Mom and Dad," she said.

Her dad beamed. "Hello, my sweetheart."

They embraced, and it seemed like forever before Emmie pulled back.

They looked the same as the last time she saw them before leaving for California, except now without the sad faces. Her mom's dark brown hair was still cut short and curly, and she still wore a white shirt with beige slacks that had always reminded her of something an archaeologist might wear. An occult explorer.

"We're so happy to see you." Her dad looked as if he'd lost some weight after she'd left town.

They'd been healthy when they died...

"We waited for you." Her mom reached out and took her hand. "We knew you would come, eventually."

"Sorry it took me so long." Emmie glanced back at the car. Sarah was watching them with a bright smile. "It took me a while to accept..."

"We know." Her mom squeezed her hand. "And it's okay."

"Victor's dead... or gone, anyway. Well, I guess he was *always* dead." Emmie gave a tearful laugh. "I know what you were trying to do now."

"I'm happy you finished what we started."

"Your friend, Betty, helped us too. She didn't survive, though. Josephine..."

"We know. Betty was a bit rough, but such a powerful woman, and fighting the good fight."

"I thought Josephine might have trapped her spirit too."

"No. Betty was old, but a woman to be reckoned with.

Josephine ended her physical life, but nothing could keep down Betty's spirit."

"I guess there's still a lot I need to learn. Betty showed me how much good one person can do, and I'm glad I had a chance to meet her. I see that it's my destiny I'll always see ghosts." Emmie glanced back at Sarah, still watching patiently from the car. "If you remember my friend, Sarah, from high school, she just discovered she has a gift too. I'm trying to help her through it, like a mentor, but she's really the one inspiring me. I won't run away from it anymore."

"There's a lot you can accomplish."

"I know." Emmie stared into the eyes of her parents. "Sarah can..." The words didn't come so easily now. "... release your spirits from this place, so you can move on when you're ready."

Her parents smiled. "No need for that," her dad said. "We were only waiting for you to return, hanging on for one last chance to talk with you, and we accomplished that."

Emmie's eyes filled with tears and her heart ached. "I love you, Mom and Dad. I wish I could have stopped the accident from happening."

"There is no use looking back. We are fine. And we are glad that you know we did our best, but now it's time to move on." Her mother caressed her face. "You will make plenty of mistakes too, but you'll be so strong, and you'll grow."

Her dad pressed her shoulder, and she inched closer to him. "I'm proud of you, Emmie. Whatever you decide to do, don't be afraid."

"I'll still miss you," she said, containing her tears.

They embraced one last time before her parents' spirits lightened and dissipated into a cloud of light as they moved up into the sky. A moment later, they were gone.

❧ 40 ❧

Alice Hyde was there to greet them when they returned, although her welcome was nothing more than a stare from the corner of the room.

"Alice is over there." Emmie gestured with a nod.

"I guess she still doesn't want me to see her," Sarah said. "Or can't solidify. Ask her if she missed us."

"I don't think so."

A scowl formed on Alice's face. "You promised to play the music box for me every night. Now you owe me extra time."

"I'm sorry, Alice, but my friend needed help with something. I'll go up there now and turn on the music box for you, and then I'll play it again tonight."

Alice had no response, peering at them through narrowed eyes and following their movements around the house.

Emmie went upstairs with her suitcase and settled into her bedroom again, playing the music box, just as she had promised Alice. The girl had followed her and now stood in the doorway, her face more serene, while Emmie unpacked.

"Did you miss me?" Emmie asked.

"I liked the quiet. You didn't play my music box, so you have to keep playing it now."

"I'll take that as a yes." Emmie looked into Alice's eyes. Still the same ghastly stare Emmie had known throughout her life, but Alice's presence now felt more like that of an adopted wayward dog that had tried to bite her upon its rescue. She sensed the potential for good in Alice, but kept a little distance between them, anyway. "If you only knew what we had been through yesterday... It was a very difficult day, let me tell you."

Alice didn't speak. No surprise. Either Alice didn't care or didn't understand, but in any case, it seemed to be the best that she could do. Tolerance, rather than affection or interest. At least Alice wasn't terrorizing Emmie anymore.

When the music box stopped playing, Alice walked away, and Emmie continued getting her routine back in order. Even though she'd only been gone a couple of days, it had felt more like running a marathon. No time to unwind, either—still plenty of things to do. The freelance projects she had accepted the previous week needed to be finished on time or she wouldn't have the cash to pay the bills, and she would need to work extra hard now to make it up. At least she was earning income—and she had a place to live.

Returning to the living room, she sat alone at her computer while Sarah left to get food. With the house to herself again, except for Alice, who had disappeared now, she focused on her work in silence, and it felt *so* good. The solitude enveloped her. Maybe now things would get back to normal.

She chuckled to herself. *Had she ever known normal?*

Sarah returned an hour later with several stuffed grocery bags and a couple of freshly baked pizzas. The smell stirred Emmie's hunger.

It was almost noon. Finn would arrive soon to eat with them. Emmie helped to unpack the groceries.

Watching Sarah now, nobody could have guessed that the previous day she had lain unconscious in the cemetery grass at the edge of death. She was her usual cheerful self.

A little later, the doorbell rang and they opened the door to see Finn cradling a case of bottled beer in his arms. "Did someone say, 'I need a break'?"

"Yes, we said it." Emmie led him inside to the kitchen.

Finn handed out a beer to each of them, opening them with an opener he'd pulled from a kitchen drawer. "I think we should celebrate a little. God knows I need it." He held up his bottle after they were ready and toasted them. "Here's to surviving last night. Victory over Victor."

They clinked their bottles together.

"Let's hope the next ghost we run into isn't as dangerous as the last one." Emmie smiled "I could use a little less drama in my life."

Sarah gazed at Finn. "Did anything happen this morning after we left? Anyone stop by? The caretaker, or neighbors, or any voluptuous redheaded women?"

Emmie laughed. "You'll never live it down, Finn."

"I'm sure I won't. But, no, not a soul has stopped by, thank goodness. It was nice and quiet there after you left, and I was actually a little... bored."

"Bored in a good way?"

"Being bored is never a good thing for a guy like me. I like to keep things moving."

"Maybe we could find some lonely, single female ghosts to move in now that it's empty."

Finn smirked. "Ha-ha. No, thank you."

Grabbing their beers and pizza, they gathered around the kitchen table, but Emmie opened the windows so they could enjoy the cool afternoon breeze.

"I like this." Sarah took a sip of beer and smiled. "I think I need another week off."

"Do it." Finn bit into another slice.

"Can you take another week off?" Emmie asked.

"No. I've used up all my vacation time, at least for a little while. My grandmother's funeral is tomorrow, and that'll be the last day."

"That's good," Emmie said. "You'll get to see your family."

Sarah nodded slowly. "It will be nice, yes. My grandmother was always good at bringing us together. It's not all good, though. I'm sure some of them aren't looking forward to seeing me again."

"You? Why would anyone not want to see you?"

Sarah rolled her eyes. "Oh, it's just that some family members think I'm weird. Well, I *am* weird, but they liked me better when I was hanging around with *popular* friends and taking this whole nurse thing more seriously. They heard I moved into this place and made it very clear they don't approve. They suggested my life isn't on the right path anymore." Sarah laughed. "Maybe it's the purple hair, I don't know." She tilted her head from side to side, letting her hair swing.

"Everyone's family is like that," Finn said. "Do you think my relatives appreciate the work I do ghost hunting? They think I'm nuts."

"Well, you *are* nuts." Sarah grinned. "But sometimes I feel like I'm a real freak."

"We're a different bunch, all right." Emmie laughed. "But I'm happy to know both of you."

"Thank you." Finn nodded once. "And I'm happy to know you, too. It's been quite an adventure so far."

"I hope we can handle whatever comes next."

"Betty said the ghosts would always find you." Finn took a sip of beer. "So we better get ready for more fun times."

"There was so much stuff we could have used in her house," Emmie said, losing her smile. "I just didn't have the time to grab any of it, though she gave me the key. Now the house will be swarming with police or relatives or who knows what..."

"We just need to pace ourselves," Sarah said.

Finn scoffed. "I'm not saying that what we went through yesterday was easy, but that's the kind of thing I'm looking for in my life. Adventure, not routine."

"That's the point," Emmie said. "We've played it by ear, but we should prepare ourselves for the next encounter, like my parents tried to show me. We never know what we might run into. Let's find someone who can train us, or at least give us some advice—someone like Betty."

"I don't know any ghost gurus," Finn said. "At least not any I would take seriously."

"Finn," Sarah said suddenly. They looked at her. "Finn, it wasn't true, what Josephine said. Your brother... he wasn't in that hole."

Quick, strong emotion passed over his face as he lowered his beer and paused a moment before speaking. "Sorry, I never told you about Neil. When you asked me why I was obsessed with ghosts earlier, I just couldn't say it."

"It's okay." Sarah reached out and rubbed his arm.

Finn stopped and ran a hand through his hair as he looked away, perhaps to hide his tears. "He died a few years ago by suicide, a shotgun blast." His voice cracked a little as he went on. "And it was a particularly gruesome discovery for my parents, to find him like that in the basement of our house. I know they never got over it." He gave a deep sigh, his eyes lost again. "I never knew he was so unhappy. I just didn't know. We were so close, but he was always kidding around."

Silence filled the air between them. After a moment, Finn continued.

"And where did he go, really? You know, you hear all the stories about heaven and hell and what might happen to someone when they kill themselves." He looked at them. "And I wonder if he passed into the sky like a blazing ball of laughter, like he deserved, or if he's stuck somewhere because he killed himself. I want to know, and if he's trapped, then I want to free him."

"We could go visit where he died, if you want," Emmie said softly.

"I'm not sure I could do that yet. I don't think I'm ready for the answer." He turned away and wiped his cheek.

She longed to soothe his heavy heart, and she knew Sarah felt the same way.

Finn cleared his throat. "I knew she was lying. My brother would *literally* not be caught dead in a hole with Josephine, anyway." He took several gulps of his beer, then broke into a half-hearted smile. "Let's just celebrate today. Tomorrow we find another ghost."

Sarah groaned. "Not tomorrow. *Next month.* Or something."

Emmie nodded. "Let's at least finish this pizza first, okay?"

They raised their bottles, smiling, and clinked them together again.

Read Book 3 on Amazon.com!

Hyde House: An Emmie Rose Haunted Mystery Book 3

PLUS, get a **FREE** short story at my website!

www.deanrasmussen.com

★★★★★
Please review my book!

https://www.amazon.com/dp/B095NCPFK6

If you liked this book and have a moment to spare, I would greatly appreciate a short review on the page where you bought it. Your help in spreading the word is *immensely* appreciated and reviews make a huge difference in helping new readers find my novels.

All FREE on Kindle Unlimited:

Hanging House: An Emmie Rose Haunted Mystery Book 1
Caine House: An Emmie Rose Haunted Mystery Book 2
Hyde House: An Emmie Rose Haunted Mystery Book 3
Whisper House: An Emmie Rose Haunted Mystery Book 4

Dreadful Dark Tales of Horror Book 1
Dreadful Dark Tales of Horror Book 2
Dreadful Dark Tales of Horror Book 3
Dreadful Dark Tales of Horror Book 4
Dreadful Dark Tales of Horror Book 5
Dreadful Dark Tales of Horror Book 6
Dreadful Dark Tales of Horror Box Set Books 1 - 3

Stone Hill: Shadows Rising (Book 1)
Stone Hill: Phantoms Reborn (Book 2)
Stone Hill: Leviathan Wakes (Book 3)

ABOUT THE AUTHOR

Dean Rasmussen grew up in a small Minnesota town and began writing stories at the age of ten, driven by his fascination with the Star Wars hero's journey. He continued writing short stories and attempted a few novels through his early twenties until he stopped to focus on his computer animation ambitions. He studied English at a Minnesota college during that time.

He learned the art of computer animation and went on to work on twenty feature films, a television show, and a AAA video game as a visual effects artist over thirteen years.

Dean currently teaches animation for visual effects in Orlando, Florida. Inspired by his favorite authors, Stephen King, Ray Bradbury, and H. P. Lovecraft, Dean began writing novels and short stories again in 2018 to thrill and delight a new generation of horror fans.

ACKNOWLEDGMENTS

Thank you to my wife and family who supported me, and who continue to do so, through many long hours of writing.

Thank you to my friends and relatives, some of whom have passed away, who inspired me and supported my crazy ideas. Thank you for putting up with me!

Thank you to my beta readers!

Thank you to all my supporters!